"Thank you for letting me off the hook, Patrick."

Ruth stood up and faced him squarely, forcing back memories of the accident that had taken away her family. "I don't expect you to understand, but thank you."

"No thanks necessary," Patrick answered tersely. "I find I don't like being a substitute."

"Is that what you think?"

"Yes—not that I blame you at the moment. But when I do make love to you, Ruth, I don't want your mind on anything or anyone but me."

A smile spread slowly across her face. "That sounds oddly possessive from a man who likes to walk away."

"Yeah." His mouth curved into a reluctant smile, more bemused than anything. "You'll have me being honorable if I'm not careful."

"And that, of course, would never do," she replied, suddenly wishing he could be content with her—and only her.

EMMA DARCY nearly became an actress until her fiancé declared he preferred to attend the theater *with* her. She became a wife and mother. Later she took up oil painting—unsuccessfully, she remarks. Then she tried architecture, designing the family home in New South Wales. Next came romance writing—"the hardest and most challenging of all the activities," she confesses.

Books by Emma Darcy

HARLEQUIN PRESENTS
648—TWISTING SHADOWS
680—TANGLE OF TORMENT
823—DON'T PLAY GAMES
840—FANTASY
864—SONG OF A WREN
882—POINT OF IMPACT
903—MAN IN THE PARK

These books may be available at your local bookseller.

EMMA DARCY

a world apart

Harlequin Presents first edition October 1986
ISBN 0-373-10921-0

Harlequin Books

TORONTO • NEW YORK • LONDON
AMSTERDAM • PARIS • SYDNEY • HAMBURG
STOCKHOLM • ATHENS • TOKYO • MILAN

Harlequin Presents first edition October 1986
ISBN 0-373-10921-0

Original hardcover edition published in 1983
by Mills & Boon Limited

CHAPTER ONE

'I OUGHT to have my head examined,' Ruth muttered dispiritedly. Again she pushed at the wings of hair which swept across her wide forehead. The swirling black cap remained a swirling black cap. All the pushing in the world was not going to change it. Her long tresses were now in a salon dustbin, irretrievably gone. The panic which had gnawed at her stomach while the hairdresser had wielded his scissors was nothing to the panic which was churning through her now.

I should never, never, never have let Clive talk me into this, she thought frantically. I'll either freeze up or jabber nonstop. Either way I'll make a fool of myself. With everyone watching. I'll feel naked. I feel naked now with my hair shorn.

A sharp buzz cut off her silent wail. Ruth grimaced once more at her reflection, took a deep breath, and, with a sense of unavoidable doom, answered the door.

'G-great! Fan-tastic!' Clive's teeth flashed white against his gingery beard and the hazel eyes sparkled with excitement. 'Ruth, honey, you'll wow 'em tonight!'

'If I don't fold up first.'

'Hey,' he drawled softly. 'You're not really uptight about the show, are you?'

'Oh no? We'd better go right now or I'll crawl

5

under the bed and stay there. I can already feel a million eyes dissecting me.'

'All potential buyers of your book,' Clive grinned, rubbing his hands in gleeful anticipation.

'You're hopeful,' she threw at him drily as she collected her handbag and the hotel-room key.

'There's no medium like television for publicity. Mark my words. Sales will be sky-high tomorrow.'

Ruth locked the door and accompanied Clive to the basement car-park, only half listening to his confident patter. She appreciated his point about publicity but was far from certain that she could handle tonight's interview successfully. A fashionable hair-do and a stylish dress would make little impact on viewers if she performed like an idiot.

Clive handed her into his new Jaguar XJS coupé. Ruth settled comfortably into the lambs-wool-covered seat and wryly wondered if owning a sports car would do anything for her psyche. She needed something real in her life, something solid she could hang onto. Writing had filled the holes, but she was well aware that it only created a twilight world for her, a fantasy instead of the reality. Reality, warm, solid reality, had died with John . . . and David. She wrenched her mind back to the present, to the interview ahead of her. She had to take a firm grip on herself and make a success of it, because her books were all she had.

The engine throbbed into life and Clive purred the car out into the city traffic. He threw her an encouraging look. 'You're worrying needlessly, Ruth. I've never caught you short of a word yet, and Brad

Parsons is the best chat-man in the business. All you have to do is follow his lead.'

'I know,' she sighed.

'So? What's the problem? Is it Patrick Hagan?'

'No.' She had hardly given a thought to her fellow-guest on the show.

'I sure wish I was his literary agent,' Clive remarked enviously. 'Whatever he writes is pure gold. All that sex and power! It's a great selling combination.'

The truth of that statement could not be denied. Patrick Hagan was the author of six best-selling novels, three of which had been made into films.

'You must be looking forward to meeting him,' Clive continued affably.

'I don't know that I am.'

His sharp glance held curiosity at her lack of enthusiasm.

'I don't like his books much,' she explained.

'They're very successful.'

She laughed at the predictability of his answer. 'I'm sorry that I'm not another Patrick Hagan for you, Clive.'

He beamed at her, pleased that she seemed more relaxed. 'I'm not complaining. Your stuff grips the heart. You'll be as big as Patrick Hagan one day, Ruth. I can promise you that. I'm pushing a good product.' He reached over and squeezed her hand. 'Just a little push tonight and your book will really take off with Christmas coming on. I know you'll do fine,' he said with easy confidence.

'With you in the studio audience I dare not do otherwise,' she retorted, releasing her hand.

Clive had shown himself willing to take over her whole life. Ruth did not encourage him. It was not that he was unattractive. He was a big, virile man in his early thirties. The gingery hair and neat beard made a vivid splash above his trendy clothes, and his hazel eyes were always twinkling with good humour. Ruth liked him. She admired his drive and energy and unfailing optimism, but they did not think on the same wavelength. Clive's high-powered, competitive world was not hers. He was nice. But not for her.

She wondered if there ever would be anyone for her. There had been no lack of men showing an interest since John's death, but their interest had been predominantly sexual. It seemed that widows were considered easy game. It was taken for granted that she wanted sex, even on the first date. Ruth's frustration was more mental than physical, and the continual emphasis on sex turned her off. She would give a great deal for an intelligent man who saw beyond her body. There was so much she wanted to share if only ... A small sigh escaped her lips. Maybe she was waiting for the impossible. Maybe there would only ever be a typewriter sharing her thoughts.

Their arrival at the studio was quickly relayed to Jean Trimble, Brad Parsons' personal assistant. She was a small, birdlike woman whose every movement carried swift precision. After a quick glance at her watch and the clipboard in her hand, she coolly directed her attention to Clive.

'Mr Atkins, I'll be taking Miss Devlin straight to the make-up room. Do you wish to accompany her or join the studio audience?'

'Ruth?'

'I'd rather be by myself, thanks, Clive.' She needed time alone to get her composure together.

'Okay. I'll see you afterwards. Good luck!' He gave her a grin and a cheery wave as he moved off down a separate corridor.

Jean Trimble strode out briskly and Ruth fell into step beside her.

'You'll have twenty minutes in make-up and then I'll take you to the ante-room where you'll wait until I call you to go on. Any questions?'

'No.'

'I like your dress. It'll look good on camera.'

'Thank you.'

Ruth had been warned not to wear red or white. The violet and aqua tones of the Pucci dress she had bought were obviously acceptable. It had been a wildly extravagant choice, but the jewel-like colours seemed to glow against her tanned olive skin and the beautiful silk clung to her curves in a perfect fit. She had not needed Clive's advice to spare no expense. The dress itself had been temptation enough.

'In here.'

Jean Trimble opened a door and led the way into the make-up room. The beautician was quickly introduced and Jean watched speculatively as Ruth was settled in front of the mirror.

'Give Miss Devlin the full star treatment, Bev. I think they'll balance out very well.'

Having delivered her instructions she made an abrupt departure, without giving either girl time to comment. Ruth glanced doubtfully at the array of cosmetics which Bev was lining up. The number of butterflies in her stomach increased alarmingly. She did not want to look theatrical. It was bad enough that she would probably make a fool of herself. She did not have to look a fool.

'What did Miss Trimble mean by that?' she asked warily.

Bev flashed her a good-natured smile. 'I'm to give you the glam treatment. Won't be hard. You've got lovely eyes and good bones.'

'Bones?' Ruth mumbled as cleansing cream was liberally applied to her face.

'Facial structure. You know, cheeks, nose, jaw-line, eyebrows. If they're irregular it means corrective work.'

Ruth waited until the cream was wiped off and then remarked cautiously, 'Actually I don't like a lot of make-up.'

'Don't worry. I won't overdo it,' Bev assured her, and started with a foundation base. 'First of all you have to understand that your face needs more colour to counteract the bright television lights. Then obviously we can't have your dress the focus of attention. Your eyes are the important feature and must be emphasised. And besides all that, Jean doesn't want Patrick Hagan outshining you.'

It seemed an odd comment, arousing Ruth's curiosity. 'Is he terribly dashing or something?'

'Dashing and something!' Bev grinned, and rolled her eyes for added emphasis. She reached for another pot of colouring and kept working as she elaborated. 'He's gorgeous! One of the sexiest men I've ever slapped pancake on, and I've seen quite a few pass through this studio. They talk about women with a come-hither look, but oh boy! And that American drawl . . . pure bedroom!'

Ruth laughed and some of her tension eased. She had not actually pictured the man in any way, but somehow she had not expected him to be attractive. If he was such a lady-killer it certainly explained why he always wrote of women as bedmates and little else.

'You want to watch him,' Bev warned jokingly. 'Charming and sexy he is, but I reckon he'd be as slippery as an eel. He had two women in here with him when I was doing his face and they were carrying on a treat with Patrick darling this, and Patrick darling that. They couldn't wait to lay their eager little hands on him, and you know what?'

'What?' Ruth smiled, amused by the gossip.

'He didn't give a damn! He winked at me in the mirror as if it was all a joke. I bet he only has to snap his fingers to get a woman into bed. Come to think of it, I wouldn't have minded myself.'

Well, I'd mind, Ruth added privately. Such men held women in contempt. It was all so easy for them, they did not care. Bev prattled on, enjoying her subject. Finally she stopped and eyed Ruth critically in the mirror.

'Right,' she nodded with satisfaction. 'Now the mouth. Hold still.'

Ruth's blue eyes had been heavily accentuated and her long black lashes looked positively false after a thick application of mascara. Her cheekbones were deliberately highlighted to give a slightly oriental look, and Ruth would never have chosen to wear the plum-red lipstick which Bev was skilfully applying.

'There you are!' The plastic cape was whipped away as Bev smiled her triumph. 'See! The make-up complements your dress perfectly.'

Ruth had to admit that the effect was certainly dramatic and quite stunning. Her confidence received a much-needed boost. She might not 'wow' the viewers but at least she looked good. She smiled at the beautician. 'Thanks, Bev.'

Jean Trimble swept in, her sharp eyes giving Ruth a quick examination. 'Good work, Bev. Ready?' she asked Ruth and gestured her impatience to go. As Ruth accompanied her, more instructions were rapped out. 'I'll put you with Mr Hagan in the ante-room. You're not on until the second half of the show. You'll have time to get to know each other before you face the cameras. I'll cue you when it's time to move. Okay?'

'Yes, thank you,' Ruth murmured.

She won an encouraging smile as Jean Trimble knocked on a door and opened it. Three pairs of eyes swivelled around and fastened on Ruth.

'Ah, Mr Hagan, I'm afraid your friends will have to leave you now if they wish to join the studio audience for the show. Do you mind, ladies?'

The clipped tone of voice brooked no opposition. Two expensive and very sleek women reluctantly detached themselves from the man between them. He was younger than Ruth had anticipated, perhaps in his late thirties, tall and lean, dressed casually in body-hugging clothes which emphasised his athletic physique. An unruly mass of black curls grew down to his collar, framing a face which would always draw attention. It was a strong face, the nose a little hawkish, chin aggressively chiselled, eyebrows slightly arched as if perpetually throwing out a challenge. For a brief moment there was surprise in the darkly brilliant eyes. Then they glinted in appreciation as they swept over Ruth.

His two female companions were also appraising her, but their eyes were cold. With a few honeyed words to Patrick Hagan they made a graceful departure, looking somewhat askance at Ruth as they brushed past.

'Cats!' she thought dismissively and turned her attention back to the man.

'Miss Devlin, I'd like you to meet Patrick Hagan. Mr Hagan, your fellow-guest on the show, Ruth Devlin. Please make yourselves comfortable.'

Jean Trimble turned and left, satisfied that everything was under control. Ruth was not quite so confident. Patrick Hagan advanced on her, brown eyes gleaming mischievously.

'I'm very pleased to meet you,' she murmured politely.

'The pleasure is all mine.'

The voice was deep and attractive, perfect white teeth flashing in a roguish smile. As his hand closed over hers Ruth was jolted in a way she had never thought possible. The man seemed to exude sheer animal attraction. A slight sensual movement of his lips showed he was well aware of his own magnetism.

'Not at all,' she retorted quickly to cover her momentary disquiet. 'It's very interesting to meet the man behind the books.'

'It's more than interesting to meet a woman who's clever as well as beautiful.'

Oh brother! Ruth thought caustically. He was gorgeous all right, right up to his glib tongue. 'Don't be fooled by the studio make-up, Mr Hagan. I'm not beautiful.' She glanced down pointedly and then raised a delicately arched eyebrow. 'May I have my hand back?'

His thumb deliberately caressed her skin, making the release as slow as possible while his eyes twinkled down at her with devilish amusement. 'You don't deny being clever.'

Ruth almost snatched her hand away, resenting the playful intimacy. 'Oh, I'm not dumb, Mr Hagan. I'll thank you to remember it,' she said silkily.

With the contact broken she moved away and settled in a nearby armchair. He casually propped himself against a table. Taking his time, in an infuriating way, he ran his eyes over her, lingering on the full thrust of her breasts and the shapeliness of her long legs.

Ruth bristled with antagonism. The last thing she needed right now was to be undressed. Resentment sharpened her tongue. 'Are you quite finished or would you like me to stand up and turn around?'

He grinned unashamedly. 'You pack quite a punch for a lady author. I was expecting something quite different.'

'Really?' Her voice was dry and uninterested, but he was unabashed. 'You're exactly what I expected,' she added with a bit more bite.

His mouth quirked in amusement. 'I'm glad I don't disappoint you.'

Ruth had an irresistible urge to wipe the smugness

from his face. 'Actually I didn't think of you at all except as a name. Bev, the make-up girl, gave me a running commentary while she did the artwork on my face. Gorgeous, sexy, slippery as an eel, would be a brief summary. She omitted quite a few other points.'

'Which are?'

She smiled her very best Mona Lisa smile. 'I keep my best descriptive words for my writing. Your imagination is quite vivid, Mr Hagan. I'll let you supply them.'

He laughed, his eyes slightly hooded as thick lashes veiled their expression. Ruth had the impression they were watching her with intense speculation.

'I must get hold of your books and read them,' he mused. 'Clearly I've been missing something.'

'I doubt that you miss much, Mr Hagan. Your own books show a vast knowledge of the world.'

'You've read them?'

'A couple,' she nodded.

'They didn't grab you enough to want to read more?' he asked perceptively.

She shrugged. 'The plots were very clever.'

He raised a sardonic eyebrow. 'But?' At her hesitation he swiftly added, 'Come now, Miss Devlin. Be frank. You're dying to tell me what you didn't like about them.'

'On the contrary,' she replied warily. 'You're the one pursuing the subject. You have no need of my opinion. Your appeal to the general public speaks for itself.'

His eyes danced at her, mocking the evasion. 'I am

more fascinated by the minute. Please. Restraint bores me.'

I'm sure it does, Ruth thought cynically and decided to take the opportunity to put him down a peg. 'When I read a book I prefer to like someone in it. Your characters are well drawn but unlikeable. They don't inspire sympathy, so I don't care what happens to them. It's simply a matter of personal taste.'

'Point taken,' he said nonchalantly. 'Did anything else stir your disapproval?'

She frowned, not wanting to be too tactless. He pushed his hands into his pockets and studied her lazily.

'Miss Devlin, I am sick to death of gushing compliments. Do please continue.'

'If you must know,' she sighed, wrinkling her nose unconsciously as she spoke, 'I found all the sexual detours very tedious. I had to skip endless pages to get on with the story.'

His grin was pure wickedness. 'When I think of all the interesting variations I poured into those sexual detours!'

'Well, they were all so clinical!' Ruth protested. 'None of the characters' emotions were involved, just straight anatomy.'

He chuckled, and Ruth found herself responding to his good humour with a smile. His eyes were quick to note her softening, and a gleam of satisfaction crept into them.

'I would like very much to continue this conversation. Will you have dinner with me after the show?'

The invitation took her by surprise, and she was

momentarily flattered by it. Then she returned to earth with a thump. 'Aren't you forgetting something, Mr Hagan?' she asked sweetly.

His frown was idle mockery. 'I don't think so. We've been properly introduced. You've expressed an interest in meeting me. I enjoy listening to your refreshing views. What impediment is there?'

'Perhaps I underestimate your appetite for female company. Most men would find two women enough to entertain.'

His hand waved dismissively. 'A temporary burden, I assure you. It was their own idea to come and watch the show. The dinner invitation is for you alone.'

His eyes caressed her with a possessive glint which made her skin prickle. For one mad moment Ruth was tempted. Then common sense prevailed and she shook her head.

'No, thank you.'

'Why not?'

'I don't think I'm quite your style, Mr Hagan. You've been misled by this prettied-up version of me. It's strictly for the benefit of the camera. I'm not beautiful or sophisticated like your friends, and I definitely wouldn't live up to your expectations.

He looked at her quizzically, undaunted by her refusal. 'I'm not the type of person to judge a book by its cover. You don't strike me as that type either.'

'You forget I've read your pages, Mr Hagan,' she retorted. 'I suspect you have a one-track mind concerning women. It's lined with beds and it's not a road I care to travel.'

The door was suddenly pushed open and Jean

Trimble's birdlike face peered around it. 'Time to go. Please follow me and be as quiet as possible. No more talking until you're on the show.'

Ruth stood up and nervously smoothed her dress over her hips. She caught the edge of Patrick Hagan's knowing smile out of the corner of her eye, and her heart plummeted. It had been reckless of her to put him offside when they were about to make a public appearance together. As they walked along she was very much aware of his easy confidence. He had a personal charisma which would show up well on television. Doubts about her own ability to shine multiplied by the second. She gritted her teeth and concentrated on steadying her leaping pulse.

The cameras were focused on a singing group as they arrived on the set. Jean Trimble indicated the hazards of cables running across the floor and led them over to the armchairs on either side of Brad Parsons. His homely face creased into a comforting smile as he nodded a silent greeting. He watched while his personal assistant checked the grouping and waited until she gave a thumbs-up sign. Then he leaned over and patted Ruth's hand.

'Relax. I'll attack Patrick first. He's an old campaigner,' he whispered.

She looked into friendly, crinkling eyes and sighed. 'Does it show?'

'No. You look beautiful. Just take it easy. I'll lead you,' he reassured her.

The 'on' signal flashed, and without missing a beat he moved smoothly into an introductory spiel for the camera. After a few casual lead-in questions he concentrated on his more famous guest, and Ruth had to admire Patrick Hagan's performance. His slightly racy anecdotes amused the audience, particularly as he invariably linked famous people to his travelling escapades. There was a wicked punch in some of his comments as he described the personal quirks of various stars he had met. He entertained, and Ruth hoped desperately that she would not provide too much of an anticlimax.

The moment came. Brad Parsons shifted his posture, turning towards her with one of his trademark hand gestures, a casual flip-flop movement which emphasised the change in direction. Ruth stiffened. She imagined her family, friends, all her school pupils and countless other people watching her with eager eyes. It was a daunting thought, and her own eyes sought blindly for Clive, sitting somewhere in the studio audience.

'In sharp contrast to Patrick, you've travelled very little, Ruth. One holiday trip to Japan, wasn't it?'

'Yes,' she swallowed nervously, knowing that she had to pull herself together.

'Do you feel that your experience of life has been severely limited by Australian boundaries?'

'In some ways, of course. To experience different cultures at first hand must be very stimulating, but I think people are much the same under the skin. They all feel love and hatred, maybe towards different things and for different reasons, but human emotion remains the same.' Oh God, she thought miserably, now I'm prattling. She took a deep breath and added, 'I don't see myself as being handicapped by a lack of travel.'

'But do you have a yearning for other places?

Patrick here seems to have the heart of a gypsy, always going on to something new. Do you have similar inclinations?'

'No, I don't think so,' she shrugged. 'Wherever you go you take yourself with you. I'm content where I am.'

'And you're at present teaching at a co-educational High School.'

'Yes,' she nodded.

'You were convent-educated yourself.'

'Yes.'

'Do you think it better that schools be segregated or co-educational.'

Her choked answers were no good. Brad Parsons was prompting for more. All right, she told herself sternly, give them something controversial. She plunged in recklessly. 'I'm opposed to segregation. It's basically antisocial and gives rise to the worst kind of sexism.'

She could almost feel the ripple of interest from the audience. She breathed more easily.

'In what way, Ruth? I went to an all-male school myself, and I think I have a reasonably healthy outlook towards the opposite sex.'

Brad Parsons acknowledged the amused titters with a wriggle of his fingers. Ruth smiled and waited for the focus of interest to return to her.

'Do you mean to say that you didn't view every girl as a sex object?'

'My word, I did! I consider that very healthy.'

Outright laughter greeted his facetious answer.

'And did you enjoy being a sex object yourself?' Ruth asked slyly.

'If only I could be so lucky!' he moaned with exaggerated mournfulness, his hands gesturing haplessly towards his portly body.

It brought the house down. He winked at Ruth and she laughed. It was more from relief than amusement. The last few questions and answers had broken the ice and she resolved to be completely uninhibited in her responses from now on. When the hubbub subsided Brad Parsons continued more seriously.

'However, I do take your point. You actually explored this problem very dramatically in your first book, *The Primrose Paths*.'

'Precisely. When a boy or girl has been forced along the straight and narrow for an unnatural length of time, most of them rush headlong into unexplored territory at the first brush with freedom. I think it causes a lot of disillusion and unhappiness.'

'I was fascinated by one of your characters, the college professor who preyed on innocence. Was he drawn from real life? I ask because I find it hard to imagine that anyone could be seduced by a man simply saying, "I want you".'

'That part of it was real enough. It happens,' Ruth assured him with a wry smile. 'It does sound too easy, doesn't it? But if a man keeps saying, "I want you," a naïve girl is drawn in by the ego-trip of her own desirability. The man need not be particularly attractive in himself. It's the girl's vulnerability which traps her. A student from a co-ed school would laugh it off unless she was truly attracted.'

'May I ask if you speak from experience or

observation? Or is that too personal a question?' Patrick Hagan suddenly intervened.

By now, Ruth was so caught up in the heady pleasure of being well received by the audience that a personal question did not bother her. That it came from Patrick Hagan only made it more of a challenge to answer.

'Both,' she stated, her eyes dancing merrily.

Brad Parsons pounced on the opening. 'Would you elaborate?'

She smiled. 'Well, from a purely feminist viewpoint I was angry that such a cynical approach was so successful. When it was tried on me I had the rather malicious pleasure of enumerating the many reasons why I didn't want him.'

She could not resist a telling look at Patrick Hagan, who immediately grinned back at her.

'Did it knock him back on his heels?' he asked.

'No. He just went on to more promising material.'

'Silly man!'

Ruth laughed. The flirtatiousness of his remark stirred an avid interest in the audience, and she quickly sobered as those vibrations reached her. She pointedly turned to Brad Parsons for his next lead.

'And your new book, *Ladies in Waiting*; I haven't had the chance to read it yet, but I'm told it covers more mature relationships,' he prompted.

'I'm not sure I'd say that,' Ruth answered thoughtfully.

'What are the ladies waiting for?' Patrick Hagan asked, apparently determined to get into the act.

'For their needs to be fulfilled.'

'And for that do they depend on men?' he continued irrepressibly, cutting out the interviewer.

'Not necessarily,' she answered, taking the bait and determined to throw it back in his face. 'We're interdependent, Mr Hagan. No man is an island and neither is a woman. We all depend on someone for something, some of the time. We rarely get what we want, but that doesn't stop us secretly waiting for it.'

'And what are you secretly waiting for?'

'I think I'll keep that my secret,' she smiled.

'What about you, Patrick?' Brad Parsons asked pertinently. 'What are you waiting for?'

'I'm waiting impatiently to get my hands on Miss Devlin's books. They sound fascinating.'

'There you are, ladies and gentlemen, an accolade indeed from a best-selling author, Patrick Hagan, to our own Ruth Devlin.'

The applause was deafening. Ruth flushed with pleasure and stole a quick look at Patrick Hagan, whose last remark had surprised her with its public generosity. He smiled back at her complacently. Brad Parsons wound up the show with his usual aplomb, thanking his guests, the studio audience and the nationwide viewers. As the theme music faded out he turned to her with an appreciative grin.

'Remind me to ask you on again, Ruth. Shaky start but a great finish.'

'I'll probably slit my throat tomorrow for saying half the things I said.' She glanced over to Patrick Hagan and added, 'It was kind of you to say that.'

His eyes took on a speculative gleam. 'I'm afraid I spoke a half-truth, Miss Devlin. I'd much prefer the author. I find the sound of her even more fascinating, and I'm secretly waiting for a change of mind.'

The sheer arrogance of the man caught her breath. Then she laughed. He was arrogant all right, but she had enjoyed crossing swords with him. If his arrogance had not been based on the strong sexuality he was projecting, she might have accepted. As it was, any further association with him would be playing with fire.

'I'm sorry to disappoint you,' she smiled.

'I doubt that you'd do that.'

Brad Parsons' face held a quizzical expression as he looked from one to the other. 'Is it my imagination or is there electricity crackling around my head?' he drawled in dry amusement.

'A short circuit, I'd say, Mr Parsons,' Ruth declared lightly. 'It's what usually happens when a positive charge meets a negative one. Definitely negative.'

'Ah!' he nodded, his eyes twinkling his appreciation of the quick-witted thrust. 'How does that strike you, Patrick?'

'Apparently I'm shot down in flames,' he grinned. 'But I'm one of the world's survivors. I thrive on challenges.'

'The challenge is in your own mind, Mr Hagan,' Ruth said silkily. 'I'm just passing by.'

'And you wouldn't like to stumble?' he suggested, again using that provocative movement of the lips.

Her eyes mocked him. 'I stopped grazing my knees in adolescence, and I have a distinct aversion to crowded streets.'

Brad Parsons almost choked. He came up spluttering. 'Oh, damnation! Here comes Jean, and I'm going to miss the ending.'

'This is the ending,' Ruth insisted.

'I saw it as a beginning myself,' Patrick Hagan declared with the air of a man about to join battle.

Fortunately Jean Trimble arrived just then and broke the intimacy of the group. After a few professional comments to Brad Parsons she took over, conducting Ruth and Patrick from the set with the intention of delivering them back to the make-up room. Ruth was glad to go. The exhilaration had died with the spotlight.

CHAPTER TWO

RUTH was silently brooding over her outspokenness as they emerged into the corridor adjacent to the set. Before she could take evasive action, Clive swooped on her, enveloping her in an exuberant bear-hug and swinging her off her feet.

'You were bloody marvellous!' he boomed in her ear. 'In my wildest expectations I didn't imagine you'd give out like that. Ruth, baby, you were an agent's dream.'

'Don't call me baby, and put me down for goodness' sake. I've just come to the conclusion that I was a garrulous idiot,' she said with some asperity.

'Nonsense!' he declared, setting her on her feet.

'Huh! You don't have to face a classroom of adolescents.'

'True, but just think of a storeful of eager buyers,' he grinned. Having expressed his satisfaction, he directed a respectful glance at Patrick Hagan, who was looking on with interest. 'You were great too, Mr Hagan. You'll have to forgive me for being prejudiced towards my favourite client.'

'Perfectly reasonable,' he said smoothly. 'You're Miss Devlin's agent?'

'Clive Atkins,' he announced, offering his hand.

'Patrick darling! You were wonderful!'

The female adulation arrived in a flurry of hugs and kisses and even more extravagant compliments.

Ruth caught Jean Trimble rolling her eyes back in impatience and smiled her commiseration.

'We can find our own way, Miss Trimble. Thanks for your time and attention,' she said politely.

'Sure?'

Ruth nodded.

'Okay. I'll leave you to it.'

She beat a discreet retreat, and Ruth turned to Clive, whose eyes were feasting on Patrick Hagan's private fan committee, obviously appreciating the way they expressed their enthusiasm. Ruth flicked a derisive glance at Patrick Hagan, who was slowly disengaging himself from the curvaceous blonde.

'Are you coming with me, Clive?' she murmured, giving him a slight nudge.

'Sure,' he nodded, dragging his gaze away and taking her arm.

'Hold it, Clive! I've just had a splendid idea,' Patrick Hagan declared, his voice pitched with warm friendliness. 'What say we all go out somewhere for a celebration dinner? It'd be good to relax quietly and have a few laughs.'

Ruth could feel the surge of eagerness in Clive as he responded with complete predictability. 'That's a great idea! I'm right with you. Ruth?' he asked as an afterthought.

A caustic negative trembled on the tip of her tongue, but she was saved from answering by a petulant complaint from the shapely blonde.

'But, Patrick! You know we're committed to going to the Sharmons' party. You can't back out now,' she pouted. 'Everyone would be too disappointed.'

'Oh, we mustn't have that,' Ruth put in sweetly,

ignoring Clive's look of reproach. 'Another time perhaps, Mr Hagan. Come on, Clive,' she added, plucking at his sleeve.

'No. I've definitely decided on dinner,' Patrick Hagan insisted, immediately halting any movement from Clive. 'You may have a commitment, Lissa, but my time is my own. Please yourself what you do. You're welcome to join me if you like. You too, Kate,' he included handsomely.

The two women looked at each other, their faces eloquent of indecision. Lissa sighed with exasperation. 'You are mean, Patrick. You know perfectly well Scott will be furious if I don't turn up.'

'And Trevor will throttle me,' Kate put in regretfully.

'Change your mind and come to the party,' Lissa purred, her eyes promising all sorts of rewards.

Ruth was fed up with the scene. She glanced impatiently at Clive, who was rooted to the spot. Patrick Hagan sensed her imminent withdrawal and put an end to the argument.

'I won't join another crowd tonight, Lissa. Make up your mind. Now.'

The two women made a reluctant exit, but there was no disappointment in Patrick Hagan's expression as he turned back to Clive. His smile held pure satisfaction.

'I hope you're not going to leave me to a lonely dinner.'

'Not a chance,' Clive assured him cheerfully.

'And you, Miss Devlin?'

The wicked gleam in his eye openly admitted the slick manoeuvring. Pride urged a refusal but she caught back the words on her tongue. A refusal from her might prompt Patrick Hagan to detach himself from Clive, who would then lose the chance of firming a valuable contact in the literary world. She owed Clive too many favours not to be generous about this.

'Very well, but I don't want a late night,' she warned, mocking Patrick Hagan with her eyes. If he thought he had won he would soon think again.

He whipped out a card from his wallet and handed it to Clive. 'Would you book us a table there while Miss Devlin and I have our make-up removed? You won't have any trouble if you ask for the head waiter and mention my name.'

Patrick Hagan took Ruth's arm and led her off down the corridor. She pointedly detached herself, determined not to give him any encouragement. It did not deter him one bit. With insolent grace he opened the door to the make-up room and waved her in. Bev's eyes darted from one to the other, returning to linger on Patrick Hagan.

'Ladies first,' he grinned. 'Attend to Miss Devlin. If you pass me the stuff I'll clean off my own face.'

Ruth was grateful for the silence imposed by the cleansing cream. Patrick Hagan was cynical, arrogant, amoral and dangerously attractive. She figured that any social contact with him was courting trouble. For some reason she had titillated his fancy, but his fancy was obviously a very passing affair and in that she had no interest at all. All the same, with Clive as a buffer, there could be no harm in enjoying his dubious charms for one evening.

'Would you like me to apply a light make-up?' Bev asked, aware of Patrick Hagan's interest.

She threw him a derisive look. 'No, thanks. I think I'll just be me. I've had enough glamour for one night.'

Patrick's smile was mocking. 'It won't work, you know.'

'What won't?'

'I like you even better without it.'

'I am pleasing myself,' Ruth emphasised.

'I know.'

'You're wasting your flattery on me.'

'No. I'm building bricks. Who knows? They might get me high enough to peer over that wall of yours.'

'I didn't take you for a peeping Tom.'

'You can take me any way you like as long as you take me.'

Ruth burst out laughing. The rounded eyes of the beautician helped to sober her. 'You really would have done much better for yourself at that party,' she said pointedly.

'And lose the enjoyment of sparring with you? Never!'

'I'm with Clive, Mr Hagan. Please don't forget it.'

'Ah yes.' He shot her a discerning look. 'An involvement there?'

'He's a good friend. I don't like him being used.'

'He wants to use me,' he retorted perceptively.

'So long as he gets value for my time. Let's get that quite straight, Mr Hagan. I wouldn't like you to be misled.'

'I always pay my way, Miss Devlin, and no one's ever complained that I've short-changed them. How about shelving your pride and prejudice for one night? I might surprise you.'

The drawled jibe made Ruth pause, but the wicked twinkle in his eyes reinforced her first judgement of him. Clive bounced in, dispelling the intimate atmosphere.

'Everything fixed. What about transport? Do you have your own car, Patrick?'

'No. I was planning on getting a lift from you, or we could call a taxi.'

Clive frowned. 'It'll be a bit of a squash for you in the back seat. It's a Jaguar coupé.'

'I don't mind. It's a great car to drive, isn't it? Hugs the road well.'

He could not have said anything more calculated to enthuse Clive. As they walked out to the car-park every virtue of the Jaguar was enumerated with all the pride of ownership. Patrick duly admired its sleek lines as Clive unlocked it.

'I'll sit in the back, Clive,' Ruth suggested. 'It's easier for me.'

'Sure you don't mind?'

It was only a polite rejoinder. Ruth knew Clive would prefer Patrick in the front. It was easier for conversation and it was unlikely that such an opportunity would come his way again. He pulled the front seat forward and Ruth slid her body in, drawing her long legs after her. She caught Patrick Hagan's appreciative look and flushed with resentment. He crooked a smile at her.

'Comfortable?'

'Yes, thank you,' she answered tersely.

Ruth made a point of keeping out of the conversation as they drove to the restaurant. She noted Patrick's good-natured response to all Clive's questions. He was not only unstinting in his answers but also showed interest in Clive's business operation, offering suggestions which related to his own experience. Clive grasped them eagerly and Ruth felt oddly gratified.

Patrick Hagan was honouring his bargain with exceptional charm and generosity. If he was intent on impressing her, she was certainly impressed. She regretted the caution which dictated cutting short any association with him. There was something elemental in Patrick Hagan that sparked an answering vibration in herself. It was too physical to be encouraged. She had no intention of becoming another notch in his tally.

Her resolve was strengthened further when he helped her out of the car. His hands gripped her waist as she regained her balance, his eyes suggesting that a whole range of intimacy should be explored. Ruth quickly stepped away, hiding the warm confusion which had tingled in her veins. The man was walking dynamite. Any woman with her feet on the ground should avoid lighting fuses, she told herself severely.

The restaurant had the reputation of being one of the best eating places in Sydney. They were ushered to their table by the head waiter and given preferential treatment in the matter of service. Clive relished it, almost gloating with the pleasure of being with a celebrity. Ruth wondered cynically how much money had changed hands here. She hid her thoughts behind the menu as Clive chattered on, using Patrick's name with increasing familiarity. Having decided on her order she closed the menu and put it aside.

'What wine would you prefer, Miss Devlin?'

The odd emphasis on 'Miss' made her look up in surprise. For a moment she thought disillusion had hardened his expression. Then he smiled, but the smile did not reach his eyes.

'I'll leave the choice to you, Mr Hagan.'

'Is Devlin your married name?'

His gaze fell pointedly to the rings on her left hand. Ruth looked down, instinctively straightening them so that the small diamond cluster was dead centre.

'No,' she answered slowly. 'It's my maiden name and the name under which I write.'

'Oh? Doesn't your husband approve of your writing? He is significantly absent tonight.'

'I say, Patrick . . .' Clive interrupted in some embarrassment.

'It's all right, Clive,' Ruth cut in sharply. 'Mr Hagan is probably used to errant married ladies. I'm sure it's quite natural for him to assume I'm one of them.'

'Ruth!'

Clive was dismayed. He could see his bubble of bonhomie bursting before his eyes. He looked from one to the other, aware of a tense antagonism between them.

'This is ridiculous,' he declared with a shake of his head. 'The truth of the matter is . . .'

'Clive, that's my private business,' Ruth snapped.

'Oh, tell him. What's the point in having a misunderstanding?'

Resentment held her silent for a moment longer. Then in a very cold, precise voice she said, 'My husband isn't here because he's dead, Mr Hagan, and I do not care to discuss the subject further.'

'I'm sorry. I didn't realise I was treading on sensitive ground. Please forgive me.'

She nodded without looking up. The words sounded regretful, but Ruth did not care if he was sincere or not. Depression was sending out its tentacles as memories trickled through her mind. It was strange that Patrick Hagan had inadvertently put his finger on one of the problems in her marriage. John had not liked her writing. His complaint had been that she drifted off into a world of her own, a world he did not share. He had also been a conservative man. Her television performance tonight would not have met with his approval.

Like all married couples they had had their differences, but John had been warm and loving, rock-steady in affection and loyalty, determined to build a happy, secure future for them. A shudder ran through her as the remembered image of that tragic accident flashed into her mind. Her whole life had been shattered in one terrible moment, John and David both dead. She closed her eyes and sighed. She could not let her mind dwell on David. That was always too painful.

'Ruth?'

'What? I'm sorry.'

Both Clive and Patrick Hagan were looking at her expectantly and a waiter was hovering at her elbow.

'Your order,' Clive prompted.

She quickly rattled off what she wanted and relaxed again. Patrick Hagan was looking at her curiously. She regarded him with equal curiosity. The electricity which had crackled between them seemed to have dissipated. He was just a man on the move, interesting and physically attractive, but lacking any real quality, not a dependable man like John.

'What are you thinking?' he suddenly asked.

'I don't think you'd like to know.'

'Don't pursue it, Patrick,' Clive jumped in. 'Her name might be Ruth but I can assure you she's ruthless. If she says you wouldn't like to know, believe me, you wouldn't.'

'Sounds like the voice of experience,' he grinned.

Clive's eyebrows waggled expressively, and Ruth smiled. Clive had been on the receiving end of a few home truths over the years.

'I think I'll risk it anyway.'

Patrick's eyes challenged her to continue, and Ruth could not resist a slight tilt at him.

'I was thinking you're a panther.' At his quizzical look she elaborated. 'It amuses me to characterise people as animals. Clive is a bear. Occasionally he pretends to be a teddy bear, but he's really a full-grown grizzly.'

'Why a panther?'

She shrugged. 'Just an impression. A sleek, dark, beautiful predator, stalking and pouncing, taking what you want and leaving the rest to fate.'

He mulled over her words and then raised a sardonic eyebrow. 'Beautiful?'

'Beautiful,' she confirmed nonchalantly. 'No false modesty, please. You're aware of it, just as I'm aware that I'm not beautiful. You were flattering me earlier tonight, but I don't bother flattering anyone.'

'So I noticed.'

'I wish someone would call me beautiful,' Clive sighed, sparking off a burst of laughter.

Their food and wine arrived and the conversation veered to less personal subjects. Several times throughout the meal Patrick Hagan attempted to draw her out, probing for answers. Ruth blocked him or sidestepped, using Clive as a cover. It amused her to frustrate his efforts to pin her down. They had reached the coffee stage when Clive left them alone for a few minutes.

'What are you doing tomorrow?' Patrick asked without wasting any time.

'Signing books for customers, doing some Christmas shopping.'

'Tomorrow night?'

'It depends on how I feel,' she shrugged. 'I'll probably be too tired to lift one foot in front of another.'

'How long have you been a widow?'

The question startled her out of her mellow mood. She stiffened, eyeing him warily. His gaze held hers, demanding an answer. It came grudgingly.

'Almost three years.'

'That long?' he said in surprise.

'Yes, that long,' Ruth sighed. 'Sometimes it feels like a lifetime, sometimes it seems like yesterday.'

'And you've been alone since then?'

'I'm only alone when I want to be. I live near my parents and I have many friends.'

'But no one close?'

She leaned back in her chair and surveyed him

mockingly. 'You ask a lot of questions, Patrick Hagan.'

'You've taken a perverse pleasure in skipping over them.'

'It's never good for anyone to get his own way all the time. Have you enjoyed your celebration dinner?'

'It's been interesting.'

'Worth the trouble?' she asked sceptically. 'All that, clever manipulation for what, Patrick? What did you achieve?'

'You intrigued me. You still do. Why don't you climb down from your ivory tower, Ruth?'

She shook her head. 'I don't think your arms are secure enough to fall into, Patrick, even if I wanted to.'

'Maybe I could teach you to forget,' he invited softly.

'I don't want to forget anything.'

'I didn't imagine the pain on your face.'

She made no reply, her eyes dropping instinctively to the rings on her left hand.

'I know you so much better, Ruth. I haven't wasted my time.'

The low persuasive burr niggled her. 'You think so?' she asked with a flash of irony. 'You think I can be inveigled into your bed?'

'No. You'll only do what you want to do. Tonight you wanted to do Clive a favour. I accepted that. The favour's paid. Now it's you and I. Don't pretend there's no attraction, Ruth.'

'You're not irresistible, Patrick,' she said wryly. 'I can fight it.'

'Why do you want to?' he frowned, clearly puzzled by her attitude.

Suddenly Ruth felt tired of the sparring. She dropped the guard she had kept up all evening. Her eyes held a shadow of sadness as she looked at him, her expression completely serious.

'Because you don't care. I doubt that you've ever cared for anyone in your whole life, except yourself. It comes through in your books. It was implicit in your actions tonight. What you're saying to me is, come and play my game. It'll be great fun. But you've got the protection of a very thick skin and I can get hurt. I don't want to invite any more grief for myself. I've had enough. I know you won't understand my attitude. I'm simply telling you this out of courtesy because no matter what your purpose was, you've been generous tonight.'

He leaned forward, elbows on the table, one thumb nagging at his lower lip as he considered her intently. 'You're right. I don't understand. Why should you think I'd hurt you? Can't we simply enjoy each other?'

She shook her head. 'It's never that simple. We're a whole world apart, two ships passing in the night. Leave it at that.'

'And if I don't want to?'

She smiled at him. 'I'm sure you can make it into an amusing anecdote, "The stupid woman who refused to recognise a good thing". File it under Failure.'

His answering smile was sardonic. 'Oddly enough I don't find that amusing, and I find success far more gratifying.'

'So does Clive,' she remarked drily as he arrived back at the table.

'Talking about me behind my back,' he accused jokingly.

'Only pointing out that you and Patrick have a lot in common. And now, if you don't mind, you did promise me an early night.'

Neither man protested. Patrick overruled Clive on the question of who should settle the account and they strolled out to the car. This time Ruth sat in the front passenger seat as she was to be dropped at her hotel first. It was a short journey, and when Clive drew into the kerb and braked, Ruth put a restraining hand on his arm.

'Don't get out, Clive. Thanks for everything.'

'How about lunch tomorrow? I could pick you up from the store.'

'No. I'll be too busy for lunch, although it's nice of you to offer.'

'Okay. I'll ring you tomorrow night.'

'Fine.' She twisted around in her seat, a polite smile on her face. 'Thank you for the pleasant evening. Goodbye, Patrick.'

'It was my pleasure. Goodnight, Ruth.'

The soft emphasis on "goodnight" was not lost on her, but she ignored it. Having alighted from the car she strode into the hotel without looking back. Patrick Hagan was a beautiful panther, but Ruth did not want to become his prey. Her needs went far beyond a temporary physical involvement, and he was not the kind of man to offer anything else.

CHAPTER THREE

CUSTOMERS came by in a steady stream, even forming a queue at times. Ruth was kept busy, smiling and writing until her face and hand ached with the sustained effort required. Her signature gradually deteriorated into a scrawl. The few extra personal words requested by some admirers were an additional strain on her stiff fingers. Several people commented on the Brad Parsons Show, saying how much they had enjoyed it. Ruth was conscious of a shifting gallery of onlookers, curious to see her in person. Clive had not underestimated the power of television. Today she was a celebrity.

By two o'clock she was more than ready to put down her pen. The store manager appeared at her elbow, politely announced that the session was over and firmly shepherded the people away from her table. Ruth sighed with relief. She stood up and arched her back, stretching the stiff muscles.

'Exhausted?'

She swung around to meet the smiling eyes of Patrick Hagan. Before she had time to recover from her surprise he had picked up her handbag and was steering her gently towards the door.

'I know you don't have time for lunch, but that was an exceptionally heavy session and I've organised a quick pick-me-up for you. The restaurant is only half a block away, the champagne is already on ice and the kitchen alerted for immediate service. We can be on our way shopping in half an hour.'

The temptation was too strong to resist. She needed a breathing space before contending with crowds of Christmas shoppers. The only fly in the soothing ointment was the surrender to Patrick Hagan's will. She looked askance at him, noting the smug quirk to his lips.

'I thought I made myself clear last night, Patrick.'

'Uh-huh,' he agreed nonchalantly. 'Look around you. Anything intimate about a packed pavement? My style is severely cramped in deference to your wishes.'

A gurgle of laughter escaped from her throat and her eyes danced at him accusingly. 'Clever tactics. You knew it was a weak moment, didn't you?'

'A bit of pampering never goes astray. Besides, there was a noticeable glaze in your eyes, and I didn't think your right hand would cope with a shopping bag for a while.'

'You were watching me?' she asked, amazed at his persistent interest in her.

His shrug was very Gallic. 'I had to buy your first book somewhere. Clive could only supply me with *Ladies in Waiting* last night.' Her look of surprise was met by an ironic smile. 'Occasionally, Ruth, I can be counted on to mean what I say. I do want to read your books.'

The light reproof discomfited her, forcing a reassessment of Patrick Hagan. It had been easier to view him as an insincere philanderer than to accept that he might have genuine feelings about anything. As he directed her down a flight of stairs Ruth wondered why she had aroused his curiosity to such an extent. She had offered no encouragement for any pursuit, and yet he seemed intent on having her company.

The restaurant had a subdued, club atmosphere; leather booths, dark, polished wood, and table conversation kept to a low hum. Patrick's appearance sparked off a smooth flow of activity. The receptionist personally escorted them to a booth where a waiter stood by, waiting to open the bottle of champagne. They were no sooner settled in the bench seats than a waitress arrived with two seafood cocktails. The champagne was quickly poured and at a nod from Patrick, they were discreetly left alone.

'I took the liberty of ordering for you to save time,' he explained casually. 'I didn't think you'd fancy anything heavy.'

'This is fine. Thank you.'

Ruth speared an oyster, rolled it in the smooth, piquant sauce and swallowed it with relish. It was delicious. She hungrily devoured the rest of the cocktail and washed it down with champagne. Still holding the glass, she leaned her head back against the booth and eyed Patrick thoughtfully. He had made no attempt to converse while they ate, and even now he seemed content to wait for her to speak. Her lips twitched into an amused smile.

'Very efficiently arranged. What if I'd said no?'

'A calculated risk,' he grinned. 'The odds were in my favour.'

'And of course the cost would be meaningless to you,' she said drily, waving an expressive hand to encompass the service and surroundings.

'Money is useful for smoothing the path,' he admitted freely. 'You wouldn't have walked this way for the pleasure of my company, would you?'

'What pleasure do you find in mine?'

The wary note in her voice brought a mocking light to his eyes. It died as quickly as it came, as if he had sensed the fault and corrected it. He answered with complete seriousness.

'You're very much an individual, Ruth, not a rubber stamp on you anywhere. Let's just say you have a rarity value. Only a man of no sensibility would pass you by without a closer look.'

A flirtatious reply would have kept her defences firmly in place, but his soft answer undermined them. Stubbornly clinging to her resolve, she said, 'I'm still going shopping.'

His chuckle disarmed her even further.

'I would have been most disappointed if you'd changed your mind,' he declared whimsically. 'I planned on going with you. I'm a very good parcel-carrier.'

'Won't you find that rather boring?'

'Not with you. What are you shopping for?'

'Christmas presents.'

'For whom?'

'My family. There are my mother and father, brother, his wife, and their six children. Do you want to retreat now?' she smiled teasingly.

'It'll be an education,' he claimed with a wide grin.

'Don't you do Christmas shopping?'

'For me it's just another day.'

'Haven't you any family?'

'My father lives in New York with his current mistress. My mother is presently residing in Florida with her fourth husband. I was a youthful mistake who was shuttled around boarding-schools from age five. I have no inclination to send gifts to anyone.'

Ruth frowned as she contemplated such a lonely existence. It was no wonder that Patrick Hagan was something of a gypsy. He had no roots, no loving security to draw strength from. His cynical portrayal of relationships between people was quite understandable in the light of his background.

'You've missed a great deal, Patrick,' she said seriously.

'Perhaps. On the other hand I have no family strings pulling me around.'

'Haven't you ever been tempted to marry? You've surely loved someone in all these years. How old are you?'

'Thirty-nine and a confirmed bachelor. I've never seen a marriage which I've envied. How was yours?'

The sharp directness of the question caught her unprepared. She sipped champagne while considering her answer. 'I think overall it was very satisfying. I miss the sense of sharing very much. And the belonging,' she added quietly.

'But it wasn't perfect, was it, Ruth?' he persisted.

'Nothing ever is, but if the balance is on the good side, then you're well ahead,' she stated decisively.

'And what are you waiting for now? An illusion of perfection, a dream that will never come true?'

'Maybe.'

'Why not take what's available? Take what's real now, instead of waiting for an imaginary tomorrow.'

His words cut straight to her heart, to that empty place which needed so desperately to be filled. Perhaps it was more sensible to take what was offered, even if there was no long-term satisfaction in it. At least it was something.

The cocktail dishes were removed and ham salads placed in front of them. The wine waiter refilled their glasses with a flourish. Ruth started her meal, eating automatically as she reconsidered the situation. She enjoyed Patrick Hagan's company. The attraction was mental as well as physical. Maybe she was foolish to object to an affair. Maybe she should cut loose, put her oldfashioned morals into a dustbin along with her oldfashioned hair. The idea brought a wry smile to her lips.

'May I share your amusement?'

She looked up at him with a sigh. 'What do you want with me, Patrick?'

'Why, to go Christmas shopping with you, of course. I'm sure it will be a novel experience. Have you a definite list or do we buy whatever attracts the eye?'

'A bit of both,' she smiled, wondering if his blithe good humour would last the afternoon. She would go along with him that far. Then she would see how she felt.

Shopping was fun. Even the selection of coloured silks and a new tapestry pattern for her mother did not faze him. He advised her on a new fishing reel for her brother, Paul, and took wicked pleasure in choosing a sexy nightie for her sister-in-law, Helen. The children's gifts were also considered with enthusiasm. Having become quite entranced with a particularly clever electronic game, he insisted that she buy it for her nephews. As for her nieces, Ruth had to insist that he replace an armful of dolls back on their shelves, claiming they already had enough dolls to last them a lifetime.

'What about your father?' he prompted as she declared her shopping completed.

'Dad's interests are stamps and music and I've ordered records for him through the music shop at home,' she explained.

They headed for the taxi-rank at Hyde Park, their arms laden with parcels.

'I don't know how you would've managed without me,' Patrick said ruefully as he juggled the children's presents.

'I wouldn't have bought so much. You're a bad influence,' she laughed.

'Hold it!' he suddenly demanded, stopping dead.

'What's the matter?'

'Look!' He nodded towards a dream of a dress in a boutique window. 'There's your Christmas present. You'd look fantastic in that, Ruth. Come on, let's buy it.'

Ruth eyed the dress appreciatively, loving the deep royal blue of the soft chiffon. The bodice was draped cunningly around a V neckline, a sash cinched the waistline and the skirt was pressed into tiny pleats, gradually frothing out into a curled hemline.

'Mmmh, it's lovely, but I'd have no use for it, Patrick,' she said decisively.

'Nonsense,' he scoffed. 'Stop being sensible and do something mad and frivolous. Where's your Christmas spirit?'

Before she could make any further protest, Patrick marched into the boutique and unloaded her parcels onto a velvet and gilt chair. Ruth trailed helplessly after him.

'We want the blue dress in the window,' he announced to the elegant saleslady.

'Honestly, I have no occasion to wear such a dress,' Ruth muttered weakly.

'Then we'll make one. It's obviously a dress for dancing. Tonight we shall paint the town red with your blue dress. Now you have no excuse.' He grinned at her triumphantly.

Only for a moment did she hesitate before throwing caution to the winds. It was mad and frivolous, but suddenly she did not care. The whole afternoon had bubbled with frivolity and she was still intoxicated with it. Patrick had imparted his own brand of gaiety to every purchase and she had enjoyed every moment of his company. To deny herself the pleasure of a night out with him seemed too stupid to contemplate. And the dress was beautiful. It was also incredibly expensive. Not even the price deterred her. With almost a sense of having thrown her cap over the windmill, Ruth paid over the money and gave Patrick no argument about accompanying her back to her hotel room.

'I'm crazy to have let you persuade me into this,' she breathed as she hung the blue dress in the wardrobe.

Patrick ignored her lament. He lounged in an armchair, nursing the drink he had demanded for his services as packhorse. Parcels were strewn all over the bed, and Ruth collapsed into another armchair and slipped off her shoes. She massaged her cramped feet and wriggled her toes.

'I warn you, Patrick. You'll have to hold me up if you insist on dancing.'

'A good, long soak in the bath will soothe the sore feet,' he said unsympathetically. 'You have two and a half hours to recuperate, and I refuse to listen to any excuses. Tonight we shall eat, drink and be merry in accordance with the season.'

'And tomorrow I shall surely die,' Ruth sighed. 'I have another stint of book-signing lined up. But it's the last one, thank God. Then I can go home and get back to normal living.'

'Home?' Patrick frowned. 'When are you going?'

'Maybe tomorrow or the next day. I haven't decided.'

'Don't decide anything,' he demanded abruptly and then smiled. 'The thought of losing you so soon cannot be tolerated. It's not every day one meets such a delightful companion.'

'We'll see,' she nodded, secretly pleased by the compliment. In all honesty Ruth had to admit she felt the same way. Patrick had not only turned her shopping expedition into an amusing game, but she had found his quick wit and ready charm strangely exhilarating. He had omitted any sexual innuendo from his conversation, and she could not remember having laughed so freely for years.

'I'd better get myself moving and let you get your rest,' he suggested amiably, emptying his glass and levering himself upwards. 'Don't get up,' he added as she uncurled. 'I'll see you at eight o'clock. And thanks for the afternoon, Ruth. It was fun.'

With a smile and a jaunty little wave he let himself out. Ruth sat on in her chair, rather bemused by her capitulation to Patrick's charm. There was no doubt in her mind that he was strictly a fun and games person, but the fun was very heady and it was time she had some fun.

The doorbell suddenly buzzed and Ruth stirred herself to answer it, half expecting Clive Atkins to be the visitor.

A huge bowl of red carnations greeted her eyes, and she gasped with pleasure as the messenger boy carried them in to her dressing-table. He handed her a note and good-naturedly refused a tip, saying he had already been amply recompensed for his services. Ruth quickly ripped open the envelope and scanned the note, smiling at Parick's dry humour.

'Happy Christmas. I was tempted by red roses but second thoughts persuaded me not to leave myself open to accusations of hypocrisy. Eight o'clock sharp!!! Time is but a fleeting thing. Patrick.'

His handwriting was a strong scrawl, dashing and distinctive, very characteristic of the man. The gift of flowers appealed to Ruth's feminine heart even though her brain told her that such an extravagant gesture was probably typical of Patrick's approach to any woman. All his little courtesies, the catering to her whims, the continual caress of those twinkling brown eyes; his whole manner showed a keen appreciation of female vulnerability. Ruth knew it came from a wealth of experience, but it did not lessen her pleasure in his attentiveness.

She had just decided that a long soak in a bath was

a good idea when the telephone rang. This time it
was Clive interrupting her reverie. He asked after
her day, wanting to know all about her session at the
bookstore.

'How about having dinner with me?' he suggested
finally.

'No, thank you, Clive.'

'You don't sound particularly tired. I could join
you at your hotel if you like.'

'As a matter of fact I'm dining with Patrick Hagan
tonight,' she admitted.

There was a short pause and then a dispirited,
'Oh, I see.'

'Well, thanks for calling, Clive.'

'Hang on for a minute, Ruth. What about lunch
tomorrow when you've finished up at the store?'

She hesitated, reluctant to make any engagement,
yet not wanting to offend him. 'I'm not sure what my
plans are tomorrow. I may very well go straight
home. Please leave it, Clive.'

'Would I be right in assuming your plans depend
on Patrick Hagan?' he asked rather aggressively.

'Yes,' she answered without any evasion. It was
just as well for Clive to understand the position. He
had no personal claim on her.

'I hope you know what you're doing,' came the
terse comment.

'I thought you liked him,' Ruth replied.

'That's different. He has a well-deserved reputation as far as women are concerned. I didn't expect
you to be taken in, Ruth. In fact I thought I detected
antagonism towards him last night.'

'For heaven's sake, Clive!' she cut in impatiently.

'I'm a grown woman, quite capable of deciding what I want to do.'

'In that case there's no more to be said.'

Ruth sighed, wishing he did not sound so aggrieved. 'It's only a night out, Clive. He is amusing company.'

'Yeah!' he bit out on a derisive laugh. 'Like a panther! That's your own description, and don't fool yourself that he won't pounce. But if you're a willing victim, obviously I can't deter you.'

He slammed down the telephone, clearly out of humour with her. His jealous resentment wormed around Ruth's mind, dispelling the afternoon haze of happy wellbeing. She was well aware of Patrick's predatory instincts. She had wanted to ignore them. Patrick Hagan was like *grande marque* champagne, so marvellous to the taste that it deceptively encouraged one to drink more than was prudent. And perhaps, just for once, she wanted to get drunk. Some *grande marque* champagne might possibly be what she needed.

CHAPTER FOUR

PATRICK stood back and appraised her slowly. No dress could have been more flattering to her colouring and figure, bringing out the deep blue of her eyes and accentuating every curve of her body.

'Delectable!' he pronounced, too wolfishly for Ruth's liking.

For a moment the old antagonism flared. 'Dining and dancing was the invitation. Don't count on any extras or we'll revise the menu right now.'

His face broke into a wide grin and he snapped his fingers in mock annoyance. 'Damn! I knew it was a tactical error to give that cold mind of yours time to retreat. I left you all open-hearted and friendly, and now you won't clasp me to your bosom at all.'

Ruth laughed, relieved by the swift move to frank nonsense. She needed laughter because suddenly she wasn't at all sure she wanted champagne after all. But it was very nice when it was only bubbling.

'That's better,' he declared and tucked her arm into his in the most approved gentlemanly fashion. 'Shall we go?'

'Where are we going?'

'Ah, well now, I have slightly revised my initial idea,' he announced as he led her towards the elevator. 'After more mature consideration, I decided that drifting around noisy, crowded nightclubs was not the best use of my time with you. I don't wish to strain my ears to hear you speak, nor do I want the evening interrupted by journeying hither and yon. So we will now adjourn to the Twilight Room in this very hotel where the food is good, the wine list adequate, and the music reasonably subdued.'

And which was very handy for her bedroom, Ruth thought cynically. Well, what did she expect, she asked herself with brutal honesty. By accepting his invitation she had given him reason to anticipate a surrender. And she was going to surrender, wasn't she?

As they emerged from the elevator and strolled through the open lounge to the Twilight Room, Ruth noted the attention Patrick drew from other women. He looked every inch the international celebrity. The cream linen suit had a casual elegance which only made the burnt-orange silk shirt more flamboyant. It was deeply open-necked, revealing dark curls on the tanned chest and a fine gold chain which supported a medallion. He looked rakish and devilishly handsome, and although he could not be unaware of the visual impact he made, he concentrated solely on Ruth, his eyes smiling down at her with all the anticipation of pleasure.

It was very flattering, and the coldness in Ruth's feet started to thaw. They were met as soon as they entered the Twilight Room and given a courteous escort to a well-appointed table. As they sat down a silver tray of attractive hors d'oeuvres was set before them, an ice-bucket placed nearby, and a slightly chilled bottle of Veuve Clicquot uncorked and poured into tall glasses. *Grande marque* champagne indeed, Ruth thought in amusement.

'Do you always get this kind of service?' she murmured as the waiters departed.

He smiled. 'Only when I take the trouble of arranging it. I thought you might be starving.'

'Very thoughtful of you. Thank you. And thank you for the lovely flowers.'

His eyes twinkled teasingly at her. 'Roses have a better perfume.'

'But we both know they suggest true love.' True love. There would be no true love with Patrick Hagan, only a curt goodbye when he no longer wanted her. Could she accept that? What if . . .?

'I finished reading *Ladies in Waiting* after I left you.'

'Oh? You must be a fast reader,' she remarked, feeling unaccountably shy about discussing her work with him.

'I was curious. Since you like to identify with characters I thought your own book might be revealing,' he said mischievously, and Ruth laughed at his devious reasoning.

'And what do you think you've discovered?'

'You surprised me with the depth of feeling you managed to impart. The anguish of loneliness was quite stark, too stark to have been imagined,' he added meaningly.

His perception made her feel defensive. 'One tends to exaggerate when writing, making things larger than life.'

'I'm glad you made that point. You'll have to accept that it's an exaggeration when I write of a character going three days without sleep and still remaining alert enough to negotiate million-dollar deals while bedding desirable females. It's just not physically possible.'

'Exaggeration usually grows from a grain of truth,' she suggested.

'Precisely. You've found your widowhood very lonely.'

She hesitated and then answered truthfully. 'Yes, I have. That's why I went back to teaching.'

'Why teaching? Surely there've been plenty of men eager to keep you company and fulfil your needs?'

'Some needs,' she muttered and leaned back in her chair, away from him. She looked at him and thought he had so much more than any other man she had met, and yet, when it came right down to it, he only wanted her in bed too. 'I wish someone would see me and accept me for what I am, warts and all,' she said slowly.

'There are no warts in evidence,' came the amused comment.

'No, truly,' she protested. 'Haven't you ever felt that no one ever sees the real you?'

'How do you imagine I see you?' he asked, his eyes teasing.

'Light amusement, rather sharp and very brief.'

He laughed and stood up, reaching for her hand. 'Maybe not so brief, and I always did prefer savoury to sweet. Let's dance.'

The band had just swung into a thrumming disco beat, and several couples were gyrating enthusiastically on the small dance floor. At first Ruth moved tentatively, but Patrick was less inhibited, swinging straight into the rhythm with a sensuous grace which stirred a response in her. Abandoning all restraint she followed him, weaving, stamping, twisting, her whole body captured in a beat which was distinctly primitive. The tempo increased and there was a provocative challenge in Patrick's movements as he stalked her more closely now in a tantalising game.

Suddenly another dancer bumped into her, and she stumbled. Patrick caught her to him, holding her steady. Full body contact brought a surge of desire, a swift wave of heat that was purely sexual. Startled, she glanced up into hotly knowing eyes. It flashed across her mind that Patrick had used the dance as a preliminary basis for seduction, deliberately arousing a physical reaction.

She forced a smile. 'Thank you, but I think you can let me go now. In fact, I've had enough dancing for a while.'

He held her for a moment longer than was necessary. 'You move beautifully, your whole body in rhythm,' he murmured, his eyes suggesting a more intimate exercise than dancing.

'One of my few talents,' she answered breezily, breaking away from him and heading back towards their table. 'Now I'm really hungry.'

Patrick held her chair out for her and Ruth sat down, vibrantly aware of him standing behind her. His hand brushed the tapering shortness of her hair at the back of her neck and she could not control an involuntary shiver.

'I feel quite ravenous myself,' he drawled, and signalled to a waiter as he resumed his own seat.

They gave their order for dinner and Patrick once more filled her glass with champagne. Ruth sipped it sparingly. She now realised that such a wine would give her a very bad hangover. Patrick Hagan only viewed her as another conquest. For some reason that hurt, and all her instincts told her it would hurt even worse if she involved herself any further with him. He was too attractive and she was too vulnerable. It was wiser to retreat behind a line of defence right now.

'How superficial is your view, Ruth?'

'I beg your pardon?' Her train of thought had been too intense for her to pick up his thread of conversation.

'Before we danced you were criticising the shallowness of the male point of view. It cuts both ways, you know. Most women only see me as a rich celebrity who has the added bonus of being reasonably attractive. They're only too willing to latch onto me like parasites and suck me for whatever I'm willing to give them.'

'Which isn't much,' she muttered in wry comment.

'Not in personal terms, no. It's hard to communicate with decorative but very empty shells.'

She sighed and mocked him with her eyes. 'If you use them, then you're both on the same level.'

He shrugged. 'You haven't answered my question.'

'Oh, I see you as a rich, attractive celebrity who likes to have his own way, but I'm not doing any latching. That's one queue of parasites I have no wish to join.'

'You wouldn't be joining any queue, Ruth. You're unique.'

'Indeed?'

'Oh yes. Undeniably unique,' he smiled, and the smile was that of the panther with his prey in sight.

'I'm glad you're perceptive enough to notice something different, Patrick,' she retorted, and quickly changed the subject. 'How long do you intend to stay in Sydney?'

'My plans are flexible. I had intended only staying until after the New Year. I don't suppose you'd consider coming to Hong Kong with me. Marvellous shopping in Hong Kong.'

A sharp pang of regret for something lost saddened her voice. 'I think I've done enough shopping.'

'But think of all the fun we could have together,' he added seductively.

'For a while, maybe,' she admitted, knowing it was true. 'Thanks, but no thanks. You're a sidetrack leading into unmapped territory, Patrick. I think I'll stick to the highway.'

'And where does the highway lead? To some worthy man who will offer security, be completely faithful, good-humoured and fond of children? Does that fit the bill?' he asked mockingly.

'Mmm. Sounds nice and comfortable.'

'Lacks excitement.'

'Excitement wears thin after a while. Surely you've noticed,' she tilted at him drily.

Their meal arrived along with another bottle of wine. The Châteaubriant they had ordered was delicious and the smooth claret complemented it perfectly. Ruth relaxed and enjoyed it, satisfied that she had left Patrick in no doubt of her attitude. He had accepted her stance good-naturedly, leading the conversation towards more general topics. Her mood became more mellow as the evening progressed, lulled by the wine and a false sense of safety.

'A hypothetical question, Ruth,' Patrick proposed after a short silence.

'Mmm?'

'On your very straight and unbending highway, you eventually meet your worthy man. Everything's right on formula except for one critical factor. He doesn't turn you on. No body chemistry! What will you do?'

'I think you're confusing the issue.'

'Am I?'

'If you love someone you want to share everything. It has nothing to do with surface prettiness. It's something deep within you reaching out to the other person.'

He stared at her for a long moment, his eyes smouldering with some undefined emotion. 'It's the sexual instinct reaching out. It's the strongest link between a man and a woman, and you're fooling yourself if you think otherwise.' He suddenly nodded towards the dance floor. 'They're playing our tune.'

'Our tune?' she frowned, recognising the strains of "Moon River".

Patrick stood up abruptly, drew her to her feet and hustled her straight onto the floor. Ruth stiffened defensively as he pressed her close, but she gradually relaxed as he swung her into the Jazz Waltz. His expertise as a dancer persuaded her into pliancy. The hand on the small of her back arched her even closer as he executed an intricate turn, his muscled thigh firm against hers. He kept her clamped against him, making her intensely aware of every contour of his body, the hard masculinity impressing itself on her own softness. The deliberate sensuality of his movements ignited a primitive need which electrified every nerve. An involuntary tremor quivered through her as his lips brushed her ear. She jerked her head away, glaring a protest at him. He smiled, his eyes lazily mocking her.

'Just proving my point, a very basic point,' he murmured. 'How do you explain this away?'

Her skin seemed to leap at his touch as he ran a light thumb down her spine. Her heart was drumming in her ears, and she sucked in a quick breath to steady herself. 'Response to stimuli,' she answered tersely.

He chuckled, a deep rumble in his throat as he swung her in a turn which left her oddly breathless. His mouth hovered tantalisingly around her temples, his breath stirring the black waves of her hair. 'Give in, Ruth,' he whispered invitingly.

'No,' she choked out, fighting to quell the desire which was creating havoc in her veins. 'At your age, I would be surprised if you hadn't learnt how to arouse a response. It doesn't mean a thing.'

'Your body doesn't agree with you and body language doesn't lie. How do you cope with frustration, Ruth? Have they been three very long years?'

Oh God, yes! The answer burst into her brain, pounding with the throbbing need of her body. She tried to dismiss it, to break free from the seductive trance he was weaving.

'If your husband was any kind of a lover . . .'

'That's enough!' Ruth snapped, using anger as a spur to push away from him. 'My husband was more of a man than you'll ever be, Patrick Hagan. Thank you for reminding me.'

She strode back to their table, her back stiff with outraged dignity. She picked up her evening bag and turned to him, her expression cold and remote. 'Thank you for a pleasant evening. I think it's better if we part right now.'

His hand touched her arm lightly and his eyes were apologetic. 'I didn't mean to give offence, Ruth. Please sit down. We'll have some coffee and I promise to behave. Okay?'

She was briefly tempted to accept his word, but his performance on the dance floor had affected her too strongly. Her nerves were jangling with a confusion of emotions, and Patrick represented too much of a danger to be allowed any leeway now.

'No, thank you. I'll say goodnight now. It's late enough anyway.'

'Very well,' he sighed resignedly, but instead of taking the hand she offered he reached for his wallet and dropped a bundle of notes on the table. 'I'll see you to your room.'

'That's not necessary, thank you.'

He gave her a wry smile as he took her elbow. 'I may not be a gentleman, but credit me with some manners. I always see a lady to her door.'

He made no attempt to break the silence as he accompanied her on the short ride up. Ruth fumbled in her evening bag for her doorkey, conscious of tension stretching between them. She wanted their association ended quickly, and as soon as the elevator doors opened on her floor she walked briskly to her room. Then, putting a polite smile on her face, she offered him her hand once again.

'It's been interesting meeting you, Patrick. Goodbye and good luck to you.'

He smiled and reached for the other hand, taking her key and inserting it in the lock. 'Why are you in such a hurry, Ruth? I have no desire to say goodbye to you,' he murmured, casually opening her door.

The polite smile faded from her face. She stood stock-still and said coldly, 'Then I'll make it goodnight. Goodnight, Patrick.'

His eyes gently mocked her. 'All that stiff resistance! It must be hurting, Ruth. I can't possibly leave you in such a state.'

He suddenly swept her inside, ignoring her angry cry of protest. The door thudded shut behind him.

'How dare you!' she spluttered as he took her evening bag from nerveless fingers and tossed it on a chair.

'I dare a great deal,' he muttered, imprisoning her with strong arms. 'Particularly when all the signals are flashing my way. Don't bother denying it, Ruth.'

She pressed her hands against his chest, straining away from him, but as she raised reproachful eyes, his mouth swooped down on hers, effectively silencing it before she could speak again. The coaxing sensuality of that first kiss roused a hot flood of sensations, weakening her resolve. It awoke a hunger for more, and the hands which had fluttered briefly on his chest slipped upwards of their own accord and curled around his neck.

The subtle persuasion of his kisses was accompanied by soft, lingering caresses, nothing aggressive, nothing to alarm, but a gentle moulding of her body against his. Having slowly reduced her to submissiveness, Patrick played skilfully on her senses until she was reeling under the passionate demand of his mouth, clinging to him for support as her body became boneless under his drugging touch. Her sensitised skin responded with urgent life as he caressed her naked back, and her befuddled brain did not even grasp that her zipper had been undone. The deft unhooking of her bra set off a warning light, flickering weakly in her consciousness, but she lacked the strength to pull away. She wanted the drowning magic to continue.

She closed her eyes and shivered with delight as Patrick's lips trailed softly down her throat. His hand slid her shoulder straps aside, baring more flesh for his sensuous touch. She felt as helpless as a fluttering bird caught in a wild storm, and the tempest grew as his hand closed over her uncovered breast. The sweet ache of possession pierced through her, making her gasp. Patrick took her mouth captive again, feeding her desire with his, leading her towards total surrender.

'Touch me, Ruth. I want you to,' he breathed huskily against her lips.

Her hand moved automatically to do his bidding, blindly seeking the opening in his shirt and sliding over the hair-roughened skin of his chest.

'Undo the buttons,' he commanded.

Her fingers fumbled in their haste and only then did the shock of what she was doing halt her action.

She shook her head, casting off the spell of his love-making.

'No,' she whispered shakily, reaching instead for her own disarrayed clothing.

'Yes,' he muttered forcefully, pulling her back against him. One hand gripped her chin, lifting it so that her gaze was locked onto his. 'Be honest, Ruth. You want me as much as I want you.'

'No. Not in my mind,' she cried in denial. 'I didn't mean to let you do this. Please let me go.'

'Feel! Don't think!'

He plundered her mouth with passionate insistence, trying to re-ignite the flame he had so carefully nurtured. His hands bruised her soft flesh in their urgency but Ruth resisted with all her strength, determined to hang on to the shreds of her self-respect. This was lust, not love, and all the pent-up longing in her heart would not be satisfied with such a surrender.

Anger smouldered with defeated passion when he lifted his head away. 'Why? Give me one good reason for frustrating us both like this.'

'You wouldn't understand,' she said grimly.

'Try me,' he grated out.

'Pride,' she fired at him, her face flushed with shame at her own weakness.

'Pride? You're too proud to let your body have the satisfaction it craves?'

'No,' she spat out, angry now that he was still goading her. 'Too proud to let you use it. Just for once in your spoiled, rotten life, you can take no for an answer.'

'Like hell I will!'

'That's it, isn't it? It piqued your ego right from the beginning that I didn't want you. Well, I'm out of your game now, and I don't think you'll stoop to rape.' Her eyes flashed with contempt. 'That's somewhat beneath the code of the great lover, isn't it?'

The passion fled from his face, leaving a tight, cold mask. He picked his hands off her as if she was contaminated with some loathsome disease. 'You're a fool, Ruth Devlin,' he jeered, and before she could make a retort he was gone, slamming the door behind him.

Ruth stood staring at the closed door, her mind a blank for a moment. Then slowly she regained her wits and dragged her feet over to the bed where she sank down, feeling exhausted and strangely bereft. She started to shiver.

'He's right about my being a fool,' she muttered fiercely. 'A fool to let Patrick Hagan get under my skin like that. An idiot! A blind, weak idiot!' She punched the pillow, venting some of her frustration.

Then, telling herself she was glad he had gone, she undressed and slipped under the bedclothes, snuggling up in the blankets to stop the shivering of her traitorous body. She tried to calm herself by mentally listing the reasons why such a liaison would have been stupid, but her body was not consoled.

Against all her principles, she had still wanted him. Maybe he had been right about that basic instinct, and yet the attraction had been mental as well as physical. He was a man she could have loved under different circumstances. But he didn't want love, didn't want to be involved, didn't want the ties of a deep relationship. She knew he was no good, had

known all along. She had played with fire and was
damned lucky to have got away slightly scorched.
Tears rolled down her cheeks and she buried her
head in the pillow, wanting only to sleep. She had to
shut out the whole regrettable day.

CHAPTER FIVE

A HAND touched her shoulder. In the instant before looking up, Ruth's heart gave an instinctive leap as the image of Patrick Hagan smiling an invitation flashed into her mind. Clive's friendly face blotted it out.

'Time's up, Ruth. The store manager's very pleased with this promotion. Sales have been great.'

'That's good,' she nodded, mentally chiding herself for feeling disappointed. It was sheer stupidity to let Patrick Hagan linger in her mind. He was finished with her and she with him. With an apologetic smile at the few customers who had missed out on a personalised autograph, she stood up, relieved that this last session was over. It had been difficult to smile and look pleasant this morning. She forced one more smile for Clive. 'Thanks for all the work you've put in on my behalf. I do appreciate it, Clive. I'm off home now.'

'Home? I thought . . .' He stopped, warned off by Ruth's hard look. Embarrassment made his eyes shifty. 'Ummm . . . sorry about last night, Ruth. I had no right . . .'

'No, you didn't,' she cut in sharply, then sighed and patted his arm. He had meant well, in a selfish kind of way. 'You're a good friend, Clive. Let's keep it that way.'

'Have lunch with me before you go?' he asked hopefully.

'No, thanks. I'd rather miss the late afternoon traffic. The car's packed and all I have to do is catch a taxi back to the hotel.

He shrugged good-naturedly. 'I'll walk you to the taxi-rank.'

They conversed casually about holiday plans as they strolled along. The thought flitted across Ruth's mind that she could have gone to Hong Kong with Patrick. She determinedly squashed the thought. The jet-set life was not for her. What had Patrick written? Time is but a fleeting thing. In his world everything was fleeting, especially affairs. No. Her decision had been right. But she wished the holes in her life were not feeling quite so dark and empty.

A cruising taxi suddenly caught her eye and she hailed it. Clive squeezed her hand in goodbye and she hurried away, wanting only to be alone.

The taxi ride to the hotel was fast and smooth. Ruth felt better once she was behind the wheel of her own station-wagon. She was leaving the city and Patrick Hagan behind. The ninety kilometres to Tergola were mostly expressway, and the turnoff to the beach resort seemed to come quickly. When she finally manoeuvred the wagon into her own garage she felt a comfortable sense of homecoming.

The two-bedroom cottage suited her needs, and as she walked into the house, all the pleasant familiar pieces of her life greeted her. She postponed unpacking and drifted over to the huge picture window at the end of the living-room, automatically propping herself on the edge of her desk which was conveniently positioned to take full advantage of the view.

Tergola lay spread out below her, the town stretching around the white arc of beach, guarded from the sea by a majestic line of Norfolk pines. Ruth loved this view, loved to watch the surf breaking over the headland rocks. Her gaze dropped to the swimming-pool in her backyard, the one real luxury she had given herself. The leaves floating on the surface would have to be vacuumed off before she resumed her usual daily swim.

She sighed and drew her hand idly across her clear desk. Soon it would be littered with paper and pens and cups of cold, forgotten coffee while she searched for words to express her thoughts. A warm satisfaction grew as her eyes slid around the living-room, resting lightly on the cool green and blue furnishings and dwelling on the personal possessions which marked happy memories. This was where she belonged, far removed from any frantic, jet-set life.

There were only a few days left until Christmas. Despite a determined effort, Patrick Hagan could not be pried from her thoughts. Irritated with herself for being weak-minded, she plunged into more shopping for the holidays. Her pantry was almost empty and stocked it to bulging point. She cleaned and dusted the house, arranged bowls of fresh flowers and decorated a small, artificial Christmas tree. Her presents were wrapped artistically and set aside.

This last exercise reminded her that her father's records should have arrived at the music shop. Impulsively she drove into the larger business centre of Jirrong, only to find that the records were expected to arrive tomorrow. Rather than waste the trip she decided to visit her parents. She pulled up outside their home and sat for a moment, looking out with newly critical eyes. It was an unpretentious, red brick home, decidedly middle-class. The garden was neat and pretty, her mother's creation, arranged in formal beds rather than sprawling in modern disarray. This was Ruth's background, a far cry from Patrick Hagan's world. She grimaced and got out, feeling unaccountably restless.

Tuffy set up a shrill barking as Ruth walked down the front path. Joyce Devlin opened the front door and the Australian terrier raced out, dancing excitedly around Ruth's feet in feverish welcome. Ruth bent down and picked her up, ruffling the silky head as an eager pink tongue sought to lick her face.

'You silly old dog,' she grinned affectionately.

'It's Ruth,' her mother called back into the house.

'Hello, Mum. Just thought I'd drop in for a while.'

Tuffy made it impossible for Ruth to kiss her mother hello, squirming delightedly between the two of them as the greeting was attempted. They laughed at her antics and Ruth put her down.

'It's lovely to see you, dear. Come on in. Your father's got his stamps all over the table as usual,' her mother remarked with a sigh of resignation, ushering Ruth into the living-room as she spoke.

'Well, well, well. The television star returns home. Should we have a fanfare?'

'Watch it, Dad! I'll blow on your stamps.'

His blue eyes twinkled at her and Ruth brushed back his thick, iron-grey hair and dropped a kiss on the high forehead. He waved his pipe at her admonishingly.

'You, young lady, have curled your mother's toes with embarrassment.'

'Martin!' came the quick reproof from his wife.

He was enjoying himself too much to be put off. 'She was most dreadfully confused, terribly proud of her beautiful, clever daughter, but inwardly writhing at the frank opinions being expressed.'

'I was not!' Joyce denied hotly, a flush creeping slowly up her neck. At Martin Devlin's raised eyebrows she crumpled. 'Well, just a bit. But you did look lovely, Ruth.'

'Oh, Mum!' She gave her a quick hug which was a mixture of apology and affection. 'It's all in my book, you know. That was what I was selling.'

'I know, I know. Don't take any notice of your father,' she answered in a fluster. 'I'll get you a cup of tea.'

Ruth sent a rueful look after her as she disappeared into the kitchen. 'Was it all right, Dad?' she asked uncertainly.

'Of course it was! Just the ticket! I thought you came through brilliantly. You even had Patrick Hagan interested. How did you find him, by the way?'

'Interesting and charming,' she answered off-handedly.

'Oh, you said that so casually! Celebrities coming out of your ears?'

She laughed at him. 'Come off it, Dad. You know better than that.'

'I do, I do,' he nodded his head sagely. 'You're a good, sensible girl and I'm very proud of you, despite the fact you've gone and cut your hair.'

'My hair?'

'I'm preparing you for your mother's moan, which is sure to follow the cup of tea,' he grinned.

He was right. No sooner were the tea things set out on a low table than Joyce Devlin turned to her daughter and asked plaintively, 'What made you cut your hair, Ruth?'

A wry look was exchanged between father and daughter.

'I thought it was time I had a change, Mum, and Clive said I should look more modern for the television show.'

'But your lovely hair, dear . . .'

'It's Ruth's hair, Joyce. You do what you like with yours,' Martin interrupted pointedly.

'Oh well!' Joyce sighed.

Tuffy was begging for a cake and Ruth crumbled one up on a plate and set it on the floor for her. 'You're ruined, do you know that?' The little terrier waved its stumpy tail in delight and proceeded to gobble every crumb.

'She took off with my ball of silk a while ago, the little devil. I'd just untangled the mess when you arrived.' Joyce reached for her workbag and pulled out a pretty blouse with a thick edge of crocheting around the loose sleeves. 'What do you think of this, Ruth? It's for Linda,' she added, naming her eldest grandaughter.

'She'll love it, Mum. Is it for Christmas?'

The conversation drifted along and Ruth stayed on, soaking in the homely atmosphere. Her mother was intent on finishing her crocheting, her hands never idle as she gossiped about people Ruth knew.

Her father examined his stamps through a magnifying glass, occasionally throwing in a comment. Ruth played with the dog until Tuffy decided she had had enough and curled up on a cushion to sleep. Her parents had quite different personalities, and yet Ruth had always been aware of the strong bond between them, a warm love that stretched back over the years. This was what she wanted, not the fleeting passion offered by Patrick Hagan.

Ruth glanced affectionately at her mother. She was still a fine figure of a woman, if somewhat matronly. Always conscious of her appearance, she used a light brown colouring to hide the grey in her fine, curly hair, and refused to wear her glasses except for reading and fine embroidery work. Her father showed his years more obviously. Apart from the shock of grey hair, his ruddy skin was deeply lined and he had become more portly through lack of exercise since his retirement. But there were youth and warmth in the eyes of both, and a quiet happiness threaded their lives. Those were the important things.

Ruth felt more content and at peace with herself by the time she went home. But the peace and contentment only lasted until Christmas day. She had driven her parents to Newcastle for the traditional dinner with her brother's family. They all sat around the Christmas tree for the present-giving, and one by one the gifts she and Patrick had chosen were opened, and that whole wonderful afternoon tramped back into her mind.

It had been so good, the fun and the laughter, the quick understanding between them, the shared . . .

yes, they had shared, truly shared the whole afternoon. She had wanted to go on sharing. So much. So very much. Her heart cried out for what could have been if only Patrick had wanted it too. She wondered where he was today; if he was already with another woman.

Tears pricked her eyes. She looked at her nephews, noting their absorbed excitement with the electronic toy Patrick had chosen. Her nieces were fussing around Grandma, showing her their gifts. Her brother, Paul, was demonstrating the new fishing reel to her father. They were all so happy and she had nothing. Nothing. She stood up abruptly and went out to the kitchen to help her sister-in-law set out dinner.

Helen poured out all the family news, making even humdrum details amusing, her pleasant face alight with humour. 'And what's the idea of giving me that wicked nightie?' she demanded archly. 'Don't you think six children are enough?'

Her grin showed the pleasure behind the protest, but Ruth was seeing Patrick's grin, the brown eyes dancing wickedly with warm, teasing laughter. She pushed the image aside and answered lightly. 'Oh, I thought you might need it to distract Paul from his fishing.'

'That man!' Helen laughed. 'And talking of men, are there any on your horizon?'

'No.' Such a final, negative word, no. Ruth wondered how it would have been if she had said yes. The memory of his love-making sent a shiver through her body. She reminded herself sternly that Patrick had not been making love. Not love.

'Well, there's plenty of time for you to find someone,' Helen was saying. 'No point in rushing into anything. Look at me! Married at eighteen, an old hag at thirty-three.'

'An old hag, my foot!' Paul scoffed as he came in and slipped his arms around Helen's waist. 'I still love you,' he declared, nuzzling the curve of her neck. 'When's dinner?'

'Dinner's almost ready, so you needn't start eating me, Paul Devlin,' she protested. 'Make him stop, Ruth.'

Ruth tried hard to repress the spurt of envy she felt. 'He's all yours,' she smiled. 'I'm off to freshen up before we eat.'

She had to pull herself together. At least look happy. Christmas was for happy families. All during dinner she made a determined effort to be bright and gay, sparring verbally with her brother and prompting her father into repeating his store of jokes for the children. Everyone was high-spirited and the hours gradually passed. Ruth was more than ready to go when her parents decided it was time to leave. Her nerves felt strung out, and they were stretched further by the prolonged leavetaking. She drove mechanically, vaguely listening to her parents' reminiscences.

'You're very quiet, Ruth,' her father commented.

'Just tired, Dad,' she excused herself.

'What are your plans for the holidays?'

'Another book.'

'Oh, Ruth!' came her mother's light reproof. 'You should get out more. How are you going to meet anyone shut up in a room writing?'

'I'm happy as I am, Mum,' she replied more tersely than she had meant to.

There was a short silence and then her father tactfully changed the subject.

It was a lie, Ruth thought grimly. She was not happy. And she did not want to write a book. She wanted a man to love her as Paul loved Helen. She wanted a loving home, a husband and family, babies . . . like David . . . oh God! My beautiful David! The cry tore through her mind and ripped into her heart. It was all she could do to keep driving. It was a relief to reach Jirrong and drop her parents at their home. She did not have to contain her grief on the short trip out to Tergola. Tears welled up and overflowed and Ruth let them fall uncaringly.

She had promised herself not to look at the album this Christmas, not to be morbid with memories. But she could not help herself. Like a magnet it pulled her to the sideboard in the dining-room as soon as she reached home. Her hands lifted it out of the drawer and turned the pages, touching the photographs, as if touching could make them live again. And they did live in her mind. The memories came rushing back, all the happy times, the good times . . . and David, her darling baby, her happy, loving little boy . . .

The doorbell pealed insistently, jarring her back to the present. She stood still, resenting the intrusion and willing whoever it was to go away. The bell kept ringing on and off for several minutes. Feeling none of the good will of Christmas, Ruth dashed away the evidence of her tears and went to answer the persistent summons. Her mind was already numb with

distress, but the tall figure of Patrick Hagan dazed it
even further.

'Hello, Ruth. May I come in?'

A tide of confused emotion swept over her. 'What
are you doing here, Patrick?' she blurted out.

'Visiting you. Do you mind?' he answered casually, although his eyes held a wariness which belied
the confident pose.

Ruth felt too ragged to cope with a confrontation.
His unexpected presence added to her inner turmoil,
weakening any sense of resolution. She pushed the
hair off her forehead, trying to think.

'Is anything the matter, Ruth? You look . . .'

'No.' The response was immediate. Then courtesy
found voice. 'Come in, Patrick . . . if that's what you
want,' she added ungraciously, standing back and
waving him aside.

She stood still, watching him as he strolled into her
living-room and glanced around, his eyes lingering
on all the personal items which made the room
distinctly hers.

'Very comfortable,' he remarked with a smile full
of charm. 'May I sit down?'

'By all means. Can I get you a drink?' she asked in
a brittle voice.

It was safer if he was seated. The pantherish
quality was emphasised by the tight jeans and the
navy and red knitted shirt. She did not want him
stalking around, upsetting her further with an
attraction she could not handle at the moment. He
stretched languidly in an armchair and eyed her
expectantly.

'Will a cold beer do?'

'I'd like that.'

Ruth took her time in the kitchen, calming her pulse-rate which was behaving erratically. She poured herself a lemon squash, added some ice cubes and set the drinks on a tray. By the time she carried it in she had regained some measure of composure. She took the chair opposite him and tried to look relaxed.

'How did you find me?'

'I persuaded Clive to give me your address. Before you reprimand him, I will add that he was most reluctant to part with it.'

'He should have checked with me,' she frowned. 'I don't understand why you bothered.'

'You kept bothering me,' he explained with a wry grin. He took a large swig of his beer and sighed with satisfaction. 'It was a long hot drive, but I missed you too much to stay away a day longer.' He shook his head at the disbelief on her face. 'I can imagine what you're thinking, but it's the truth nevertheless. I wanted you to stay with me, Ruth. I gambled with physical persuasion and it was the wrong move. I'm sorry about that, and also for reacting so churlishly to your rejection. Can we start again?'

'Start what again?' she asked sharply. 'Nothing's changed. I'm still not interested in an affair with you, Patrick.'

'I realise that.'

The softness of his reply agitated her far more than was reasonable. 'Do you? Do you?' she repeated vehemently. 'Or have you come here to torment me?'

'Torment you?'

His frown suggested concern and Ruth could not

swallow it. 'Don't be such a damned hypocrite!' she flared at him. 'You want to start again, but the goal's the same, isn't it? Get Ruth Devlin. Why don't you play with your own kind? Those women who were with you at the studio, they can handle the score.' She covered her eyes with her hand, rubbing the lids to force back the tears which had threatened to form. Her control was teetering on the brink and she forced herself to face Patrick calmly. 'I'm sorry. You shouldn't have come.'

His gaze narrowed on the over-bright eyes. 'Maybe not,' he admitted reluctantly. 'But it seems to me you could do with some cheerful company right now, and I'm here. Give me this evening, Ruth. I'll play fair with you.'

'Fair!' She gave a brittle laugh and swallowed the bitter emotion which choked her throat. Nothing was fair. She had lost John and David. Now she was faced with the only man who had stirred her heart since then. And he was a dilettante.

She drew in a shuddering breath and stood up. Without even glancing at Patrick she walked list-lessly over to the picture window and gazed out to sea. Huge waves crashed onto the headland rocks, sending up venomous shoots of spray. It looked wild and inviting. Like Patrick Hagan. Wild, inviting and dangerous. He had come here, still wanting her, and she . . . she needed him. She could not bear the cold, cold loneliness.

'I think I'll have a swim in the pool,' she muttered dully, not bothering to look at him. 'Did you bring a costume with you?'

'Yes, in the car.'

She swung around to face him, her expression set in irony. 'Prepared for everything?'

He stood up and moved slowly towards her. She made no protest as he cupped her chin lightly with his hand. His eyes questioned her intently and then he bent his head and brushed her lips with his, a soft, sensuous kiss, vaguely tantalising and ending quickly.

'Thanks, Ruth,' he murmured.

Then he was striding towards the door. Ruth knew it was recklessly stupid to let him stay. Patrick was expecting to get his own way, regardless of what he said. It was in the nature of the man. Wild and inviting.

This evening would be a contest of wills. At this moment she was not sure who would win. She was not even sure if she cared any more. It was a precarious state of mind to be in with a panther on the prowl.

CHAPTER SIX

'You can change in here. The bathroom's at the end of the hall.'

Ruth opened the door of the second bedroom and then left him. In her own bedroom she changed into her bikini and hung up the sundress she had discarded. Patrick was already waiting for her when she emerged, and her eyes skidded over his body, startled by the brevity of his costume. It was a mere token of modesty which covered so little that he might as well have been naked. Quickly averting her gaze, she led the way out to the back balcony and down the stairs to the pool.

Her legs felt like jelly, her stomach was a hollow pit and her head buzzed with doubts and fears. In a defiant reaction against her inner perturbation, Ruth tossed her towel on a sun-lounger, plunged into the water and swam several lengths of the pool in a strong crawl before she paused.

Patrick was still standing by the edge. He watched her intently with a slight smile upon his face. His physique was everything it had promised to be; leanly muscled, perfectly proportioned from his broad shoulders to his strong legs, every firm inch of tanned flesh declaring his superb fitness.

'Aren't you coming in?' she asked. She felt more confident in the water.

'Is it safe now?' he grinned. 'You were swimming

so ferociously I didn't want to get in your way.'

'The pool's small, but it can take two of us,' she observed drily.

It was an invitation. He dived in and came up to her, shaking the water from his eyes. 'Feeling better?'

She gave him a sidelong glance, acknowledging his perception. 'A little.'

'It's not me, is it? You were upset before I came.'

She started a lazy backstroke away from him, letting the gentle wash of water soothe her. He followed with a sidestroke, quickly drawing level.

'I was thinking of you with your family. I thought you'd have had a happy day,' he persisted questioningly.

'It was.' She rolled sideways and smiled at him. 'The boys loved their present. Everyone was delighted. We shopped very well.'

He smiled back at her, his eyes warm with remembered pleasure. 'You know, I really enjoyed that afternoon.'

'I did too.'

They reached the end of the pool and started back down.

'So what went wrong with today? Before I came?'

'Nothing. I just felt lonely and miserable.'

'And that's why you let me stay?'

'I guess so.' It was a reluctant answer and she added wryly, 'Against my better judgement.'

'That's not exactly flattering,' he mocked lightly.

She flashed him a serious look. 'Don't make me rue it, Patrick. I'm a bit off-balance right now, not even fair game for you.'

'That's a hell of a thing to say!'

His eyes were probing hers intently and Ruth swerved away, swimming underwater until she reached the steps. Patrick did not follow her out, but she was conscious of his gaze as she rubbed herself dry with the towel. It made her tense, overly aware of her own body.

'I'll bring down some drinks. We might as well sit out here. It's cooler.'

She took the opportunity to wrap a sarong-styled skirt around her waist. It made her feel less vulnerable. Patrick was already stretched out on his towel when she returned with the drinks. He looked totally relaxed.

'How did you spend today?' Ruth asked, wanting to turn the conversation away from herself.

'You've heard of Scott Hindley?'

'The movie producer,' she nodded.

'Uh-huh. I met him at the Cannes Film Festival this year. He's interested in the book I'm writing, since it's set partly in Australia. We sailed on the Harbour this morning, then had drinks on his vast patio with various people popping in and out. There was an elaborate Christmas dinner and the usual lethargy to follow.'

'And here was I pitying you because you had no family to go to,' Ruth laughed.

'You did think of me then,' he grinned.

'You're not exactly forgettable, Patrick, but I've been trying,' she advised him shortly.

'Well, I hope you had as little success as I had,' he replied dryly. 'Forget the woman, I said to myself, but you were like a thorn in my side, constantly irritating me. There I was today, in the middle of the social swim and I only wanted your company. I'd planned to come here tomorrow. I knew you'd be busy today, but damned if I could wait another minute.'

His eyes caressed her and Ruth's heart flipped over. She struggled to put up some defences, knowing she must not reveal her weakness. She looked out over the garden towards the far horizon. The sea was changing colour with the setting sun, but she knew that Patrick would never change his colours.

'What niggled you? The fact that the game ended in stalemate?' she asked flippantly.

He was silent for a long time until Ruth was drawn to look at him curiously. He shrugged.

'I was a fool,' he said with a hint of self-mockery. 'I liked what we had before I grabbed for too much. I suppose you thought I was handing you a line when I said you were unique?'

'It did occur to me.'

'Funny! I didn't realise how true it was until after you'd gone. All I could see at the time was the challenge. You threw out a challenge from the moment we met. I couldn't let you get away with it.'

'Ego, Patrick,' she commented softly.

'Not entirely. I wanted to explore you as a person too. Your thinly veiled contempt kept getting in the way. And yes, I wanted to get back at you, make you accept me. But it was more than that, Ruth.'

'Was it?' she asked sceptically.

His eyes pinned her down. 'You know it was. You could have said no to the lunch, the shopping, the dinner and the dancing, just as you said no afterwards.'

'I had my reasons. What were yours if it wasn't the challenge?'

'You had depth.'

The answer lay there between them waiting to be picked up. Ruth looked away, refusing to bite. She had always been aware of his perception, but Patrick had surprised her with his honesty. Somehow it shifted the defensive ground on which she stood, making it shaky. She took refuge in the lengthening shadows of approaching twilight, hiding her face from him. He saw too much as it was.

'Tell me about your husband.'

The request startled her. She darted a glance at him, too disturbed to hold his gaze. 'Why?' she demanded huskily.

'I'll quote you. "He was more of a man than you'll ever be".'

'Did that hurt?'

'No,' he answered easily, with no reproach in his tone of voice. 'I'm what I am. I don't feel particularly inadequate. Some people idealise the dead. I wondered if you were falling into that trap. It's not a healthy attitude.'

She considered the suggestion for a while before rejecting it. 'No. I don't idealise John. There were faults on both sides in our marriage. He was over-possessive, inclined to be jealous without cause. I was too self-contained, not demonstrative enough. There were differences in temperament, but we did love each other. Given time I think we would have worked out the problems. Both of us wanted to, you see. We wanted to build a happy life together.'

She drew up her knees and rested her head on

them, turned towards Patrick so that she could see him. 'If one made an objective comparison between you and John, you'd probably outpoint him on every point, bar one. And that is the important one. You don't want to build, Patrick. You want to take what's there. As soon as you become dissatisfied you move on. You call it freedom. To me it is a frightening emptiness. When John and I quarrelled, neither of us feared that the other would walk out permanently. We released tension and sprang back closer together. The tie was always there, unbreakable, except by death.'

'How did he die, Ruth?'

The question was gently put and there was no reason not to answer it, but Ruth found the words difficult to utter. Stars were beginning to appear in the purpling sky and the breeze was freshening. She shivered and stood up.

'I'm hungry. Are you ready for a meal?'

He swung his legs down and sat staring up at her thoughtfully. 'It's been three years. Surely it's not still painful.'

'Not normally,' she replied stiffly and forced the words out. 'It was a car accident. On Christmas Day.'

She bent to pick up the empty glasses, but he forestalled her action, gathering her into his arms and pressing her close to his heart. His hand stroked her hair in gentle comfort, letting her know there was nothing sexual in this embrace. She linked her hands around his neck and hung there weakly, accepting the strength he was offering.

'I'm glad you came,' she whispered against his

bare shoulder. 'For whatever reason.'

'Don't give me an invitation, Ruth,' he muttered. 'I want you enough to accept it, even if I have to share you with a ghost.'

He tilted her head back purposefully and there was a dark passion in his eyes. They glittered in the half-light of evening, insisting that Ruth take him as the man he was. Even as his mouth descended slowly towards hers, the challenge was still there. Ruth knew that one word would stop him, that he would respect her refusal. Instead her lips parted willingly under his, welcoming the warm invasion of his mouth and responding uninhibitedly with a wild passion of her own. She leapt headlong into a whirl-pool of sensation which sucked every thought from her mind. She clung to Patrick with a desperate need to be loved and he moulded her tightly against his body until the urge to become one communicated itself with burning intensity.

He wrenched his mouth from hers, shuddering as he drew in a deep breath. 'Why aren't you fighting me, Ruth?' he demanded hoarsely. 'I'll take you if you don't fight me.' His hands pressed his claim, moving over her in feverish possession. Then sud-denly gripped her upper arms and pulled her away from him. 'Say something,' he grated out.

She looked at him, the large, blue eyes pleading for love, her lips quivering, incapable of forming words. He sighed heavily and shook his head. She stood motionless as he undid the knot at her waist, releas-ing her skirt.

'Come on. We'll have a swim before we eat.'

He picked her up in his arms and dumped her into

the deep end of the pool, diving in after her. The water shocked Ruth back to cold sanity and she began swimming automatically. Patrick ignored her, ploughing up and down the pool like an angry shark. She was floating on her back when he pulled up next to her, a deep frustration showing on his face.

'I could have been anyone, couldn't I, Ruth?' he demanded harshly. 'You just needed someone.'

'No,' she denied quietly, letting her feet sink to the bottom. She stood up and faced him squarely. 'I don't expect you to understand, but thank you for letting me off the hook.'

'No thanks necessary,' he answered tersely. 'I find I don't like being a substitute.'

'Is that what you think?'

'Yes, that's what I damned well think. Not that I blame you for it at the moment. But when I do make love to you, Ruth, I don't want your mind on anything or anyone but me.'

A smile spread slowly across her face. 'That sounds oddly possessive from a man who likes to walk away.'

His mouth curved into a reluctant smile, more bemused than anything else. 'You're right. I'm crazy.'

'Nice crazy.'

'Yeah?' He cocked his eyebrow at her sardonically. 'Well, don't bank on it continuing. Any minute now I might sort myself out. God knows you'll have me being honourable if I'm not careful.'

'And that, of course, would never do.' She laughed as she waded towards the steps.

'Ruth.'

He had said her name quietly, almost experimentally, and she threw a questioning glance back over her shoulder. There was an odd, introverted look on his face. He was looking at her, yet seeing only his thoughts. Then his eyes cleared and he smiled. It was a friendly, open smile.

'I can toss a good salad if you need some help.'

'Then you're invited into my kitchen,' she replied, suddenly wishing that he could be content in a domestic scene.

She felt more at ease with him as they strolled across the lawn together. She did not even feel self-conscious as she preceded him up the steps. Patrick showed himself very adept at salads and he kept up a light banter as they worked in the kitchen. When everything was almost ready, Ruth handed him a chilled bottle of white wine and told him to open it.

'You'll find glasses in the sideboard. I'll bring in the rest.'

He read the label on his way into the living-room, calling back that her taste was admirable. It was a German Riesling which Ruth particularly liked. For some reason she felt pleased with the compliment. As she collected cutlery and table mats she found herself humming a tune, and decided to put on some background music for dinner. She was heading for the hi-fi equipment in the living-room when the curious stillness of Patrick's figure caught her attention and she turned, a flippant remark on the tip of her tongue. Only then did she realise what he was doing and she froze, the blood draining from her face.

Either he sensed her presence or some strangled

sound had escaped her throat. He swung around, one hand still holding a leaf of the photograph album. 'Why didn't you tell me there was a child, Ruth?'

'Don't! You shouldn't have looked. You had no right.'

The words gabbled out as she walked stiffly towards the sideboard and snatched the album from his grasp. Having slammed it shut she clutched it protectively against her chest. His puzzled expression told her she had over-reacted, but somehow his intrusion into that private, precious past had seemed a sacrilege, like an unbeliever carelessly handling something sacred.

'Why should it trouble you? The album was lying there on the sideboard and I was curious about your life. Where is the boy? With your parents?'

'He's dead.'

The bleak finality of that statement silenced him.

'He was only two years old.' Her voice shook with the loss, echoing the silent anguish in her eyes.

The utter poignancy of the moment stilled the questions on Patrick's tongue. Finally with deep compassion he asked, 'He was in the car with your husband?'

The words twisted her anguish into another painful knot. 'No. They weren't in a car.'

He did not understand, but he saw the flicker of remembered horror in Ruth's grieving eyes and he had to exorcise those ghosts from her mind. 'Tell me.'

She stared at him, not really seeing him as she recited the facts like a faulty, mechanical doll. 'We'd given David a toy sailing boat for Christmas. He was entranced with it. We drove out to the lake so he could enjoy playing with it. We parked the car and stood at the side of the road, waiting for a break in the traffic for us to cross over. David tugged his hand out of John's so he could examine the boat more easily. We were laughing.

'Before we could stop him David started running towards the water. He was so small, you see. I don't think the driver saw him. John tried to save him, carry him free of the danger. There wasn't enough time. When the driver braked, the car swerved into them. It happened right in front of me and there was nothing I could do. They were both killed, David instantly. John lingered for a while but he didn't make it. This album is all I have left.'

'It's past, Ruth. Let it go,' he said harshly, jolting her free of the agonised memory. He withdrew the album from her arms and replaced it on the sideboard. 'That won't bring either of them back. Your life is here and now, with me.'

'With you?' Her laugh had a bitter ring to it. 'Do you imagine you can replace what I had?'

'No,' he answered calmly. He reached for the opened bottle of wine and poured it silently into the two glasses he had set out. 'Here, you need a drink. Come on, we'll sit down for a while.'

He handed her a glass and nodded towards the armchairs. Knowing she was too upset to eat, Ruth went along with his suggestion. She sat down and eyed him warily, resentful of his abrupt dismissal of everything that had been dear to her. He settled in the chair opposite and leaned forward, elbows on his knees. He rolled the glass around between his hands as if intent on taking the chill off the wine.

'No one can replace what you had, Ruth. I certainly can't and I wouldn't try.' His eyes suddenly swept up and pinned her with sharp intensity. 'What I can do is offer you something different.'

'I thought I'd made myself clear on the subject of your light affairs, Patrick,' she said acidly.

He made a wry grimace and there was a shade of self-mockery in his voice as he replied, 'I think you'll have to make a little adjustment in your thinking, because I find I don't want a light affair with you at all. I want you to marry me.'

She stared at him disbelievingly.

'Obviously it won't be the kind of life you had with John, but . . .'

'Don't go on, Patrick.' She could not bear him to go on. The cynicism he had shown towards a marriage relationship made his offer too incredible. Anger stirred, sharpening her tongue. 'Did you think you had to offer marriage to get me into bed? A little twist to the game?'

He shook his head. 'I could have had you earlier tonight if that was all I wanted. You know that, Ruth. You're the only woman I've ever met that I've wanted for my wife, and by that I do mean a very permanent relationship.'

'You've got to be joking,' she said dismissively, impatient with his pose of caring.

'No. We click together. Don't tell me you haven't felt the same, because it comes across. We can share a great deal. Think about it. You needn't be lonely any more.'

His words were softly persuasive, peeling away the hard shell of disbelief.

'You're not joking, are you?'

'No.'

'You said you didn't believe in marriage.'

'I don't want to lose you. If that means tying you to me legally, that's what I'll do.'

'And of course divorce is so easy nowadays, isn't it?' she threw at him sarcastically, still struggling to accept his sincerity.

'I won't be the one to walk away, Ruth.'

The dark eyes held no spark of amusement. They were compelling in their intensity of purpose, willing her to surrender her life to him.

'This is crazy, Patrick,' she argued, too confused to do anything else. 'You hardly know me. What has it been? One afternoon and three nights.'

'I know you well enough. I'd be crazy to let you go. You're everything I want in a woman. It goes much deeper than physical attraction, Ruth. I want you at my side, in bed and out of it. I want to take care of you.'

'Don't tell me I've aroused your protective instincts,' she laughed abrasively, standing up in one abrupt movement. She looked down at him, her eyes betraying inner turmoil. 'It's a generous offer, Patrick, but you'll think better of it shortly. We're probably both a bit light-headed at the moment. Let's eat, shall we?'

Without waiting for an answer she escaped to the kitchen. His proposal had shaken her and she needed time to adjust her thinking and settle down the emotional chaos he had triggered.

'I'll take in the table mats and cutlery, shall I?'

Ruth started at his quiet voice. She had been holding the salad plates, staring blankly at them.

'Yes, thank you,' she muttered, feeling a hot rush of blood up her neck.

She followed him in and then darted back for mustard and pickles and the other condiments, using activity to cover her agitation. She finally accepted the chair Patrick was holding for her and they began their meal in silence. Ruth found she had little appetite but stubbornly picked at her food, not inviting a conversation which she found disturbing.

'I won't change my mind, you know,' Patrick declared quietly. 'The more I think about it the more certain I feel. Marry me, Ruth. We could have a good life together.'

'People don't change overnight, Patrick. You're acting on impulse.'

'Then it's the best impulse I've ever had. I think you're what I've been looking for all my life while making do with second-best. I would never under-value you, Ruth. I like you just as you are. No false images.'

She toyed with her food, her heart leaping errati-cally as she digested his words. There was a curious elation bubbling across her mind, making nonsense of the objections which were struggling to surface.

'We're too different.'

'Are we?'

'You know we are. You like flitting from place to place. I like to be settled.'

'What does it matter where we are as long as we're together? But if that's your one objection, I'm willing to settle down most of the year. If I need to travel we can make it a holiday.'

She looked askance at him, suppressing the urgent plea of her heart. 'If I marry again, I'd want a family. I don't exactly see you as good father material.'

'A little while ago you didn't see me as husband material. You're wrong, Ruth. With you as my wife I'd like a family.'

There was a surprising tenderness in his eyes which completely undermined her prejudice. She could not hold his gaze. She glanced down at the wine in her glass. It shocked her to see her hand trembling and she gulped down some Riesling, hoping it would steady her.

'I don't know, Patrick,' she muttered. 'How can you be so sure it's not a passing fancy?'

He smiled, sensing that she was weakening. 'Probably because my gut is twisted in knots waiting for your answer. Say yes, Ruth. Then maybe I could eat this meal.'

It surprised a smile from her.

'Seriously though, I've wanted you from almost the first moment we met. That first desire has increased in leaps and bounds until it won't be satisfied with anything less than a life sentence. I need you, Ruth, and I think you need me just as much. You're floating in a vacuum. Let me fill it.'

He reached over the table and removed her hand from the glass. The unexpected contact sent a light tremor up her arm and her eyes held an unconscious plea as his fingers found the quickening pulse in her wrist.

'You respond to me. You can't deny it. We can

talk to each other. Our minds are in tune. We have words in common. Say yes, Ruth.'

His eyes were caressing her with a depth of emotion which burnt into her soul, demanding pliancy. The last flicker of resistance was scorched away as the wild flame of her own needs leapt up to meet his.

'All right. I'll marry you.'

A brilliant smile lit his face and triumph gleamed in his eyes. He pushed back his chair and rounded the table, lifting her to her feet in an exuberant embrace. He laughed and it was a shout of pure happiness.

'You're mad, Patrick! You know that?' she laughed back at him, half amazed at her own madness.

'Beautifully, gloriously mad, and I love you, Ruth Devlin.' He gazed down at her in soft wonder. His fingers lightly caressed her cheek. 'I never expected to say that to a woman, but I do, Ruth. I do love you. I'll try to make you happy.'

'I've been fighting you so hard, I'm still frightened to say it,' she admitted huskily, but her eyes told him of total surrender.

'Don't be frightened, my darling,' he murmured and his mouth closed over hers in a sweet seal of commitment.

It was a long, lingering, beautiful kiss which made Ruth feel warm and safe. His hands slid up and gently held her face as he kissed her eyes, her cheeks, her nose, and then at last, her mouth again, a more sensuous, demanding possession which stirred a deep, trembling excitement. A fine tremor ran through Patrick's body as he drew away, but Ruth was too dazed to let him go. She clung to him, needing the security of his arms. His hands ran lightly over the soft contours of her body. She pressed closer, nestling her head near the curve of his throat, leaning on his strength. She heard his deep sigh, almost a groan, and his warm breath wavered through her hair. Then hungry lips sought the bare skin of her shoulders and slowly traced an erotic line up her throat, teasing her head backwards. He paused when he reached her softly parted mouth and she languidly opened heavy eyelids.

'Who am I, Ruth?'

It was a hoarse whisper and the glitter in his eyes demanded recognition. The question was oddly out of place, discordant in their harmony.

'Say my name, Ruth. Say you're mine.'

His passionate insistence was reinforced by hands which moulded her body to his with increasing pressure, forcing an awareness of his hard virility.

'Patrick?'

The name was a tremulous protest as his fingers made light work of the string ties supporting her bikini bra.

'Keep my name on your lips, Ruth. Keep it there until I can imprint it on your mind and carve it onto your heart.'

She gasped as he freed her breasts, but any words were stolen away by a questing mouth, intent now on arousing a desire to equal its own. The raw sensuality of naked skin against skin heightened the fierce pleasure of his kiss. Ruth's breasts seemed to swell as she was crushed against him, the rough curls of his chest prickling the nipples to electric awareness. He arched her against him, stirring a primitive ache for possession. Her body quivered with urgent longing and this time Patrick did not question the tele-graphed message. He swept her up in his arms and strode into the bedroom.

'Patrick,' she breathed raggedly as he placed her gently on the bed. Her eyes were large and luminous, pleading dumbly for him to release her from the sexual pressure he was exerting. Her mind told her that this loving was premature, even though her body cried out wantonly for fulfilment.

He hesitated, one hand tracing her curves in a featherlight caress. He tore his gaze from hers and looked over her, hungrily coveting what was there for him to take. With barely held restraint he lowered himself beside her and rested his head just over her heart, listening to the pounding which echoed in her head.

'Don't you want me to love you, Ruth?' It was an agonised whisper, begging for her surrender.

Her fingers stroked the dark mass of unruly curls, easing her agitation. 'You know I do, but . . .'

An intense wave of pleasure strangled her voice as his mouth closed over her breast. Then his hand was pushing her skirt aside and she was mesmerised by the erotic caress of her inner thigh. She could not find the will to stop him as he removed her clothes. Her body was drugged with his love-making, her skin quivering feverishly, leaping at every touch. Deep inside her a panicky voice cried out against the rush of passion, but it was drowned in a tidal wave of desire. There was a tiny respite when Patrick strip-ped off his own clothes and Ruth uttered a choked

sound, something between a whimper and a moan of
longing. Then his muscular weight descended on her
and his lips were on hers again, compellingly seductive.

'I can't risk it, Ruth.' It was a breath of apology, a
plea for understanding. 'You have to be mine.'

CHAPTER SEVEN

SHE woke slowly, aware of an unaccustomed warmth behind her and a heavy weight around her waist. She turned slightly and in the harsh, morning sunlight, scanned the face of the man lying beside her. The emotion-charged surrender of last night ripped through her mind on a swift wave of panic. Patrick was almost a stranger and yet she had promised to marry him, had already given herself to him.

He stirred, his arm tightening around her. Immediately her heartbeat quickened. Gentle lips brushed against her hair.

'Ruth? Are you awake?'

'Yes,' she whispered, her lips dry and stiff.

He moved so that she rolled onto her back, and she glimpsed the deep satisfaction in his eyes before he saw the fear in hers. Instantly his expression changed to one of concern.

'Don't look like that.' He rocked her to him in a fierce embrace, raining urgent kisses all over her face. 'You loved me last night. Don't change now, Ruth, please.' It was an anguished whisper, demanding reassurance. 'We'll get married tomorrow, get a special licence. If I have to keep you in bed until then and chain you to my wrist on the way, we'll get married tomorrow,' he muttered with grim determination.

A hysterical bubble of laughter burst from her lips

as a surge of love swept away her doubts. 'No, I don't think you'll have to do that,' she gasped. Her eyelashes fluttered up and the softness of her gaze drew a heavy sigh from him.

'I thought . . . Why the fear, Ruth?'

She reached up and smoothed the frown lines from his forehead. 'I wasn't sure. I woke up and last night seemed like some crazy dream.'

'A crazy, wonderful dream that I don't want ever to end. Don't doubt my love for you, Ruth. It's very, very real.' He punctuated the last few words with butterfly kisses on the corners of her mouth before taking her lips in a lingering promise. 'Feel better now?' he smiled as he drew away.

'Mmm, but I'm ravenously hungry.'

The smile turned into a wicked grin and he began to laugh.

'For food, you idiot!' she laughed back at him, pushing him away from her.

He pulled her down on top of him. 'I won't let you go until you tell me you love me.'

'I love you.'

'And you'll marry me tomorrow.'

'I can't.'

His eyes darkened. 'Why not?'

She grinned at him teasingly. 'This isn't California, Patrick. We Australians take marriage seriously. You have to wait a month and a day. That's the law.'

'You're joking!'

'Nope.' She giggled at his open-mouthed horror.

'That's barbaric! I thought this country was supposed to be civilised.'

'It is. It's only barbaric Californians who want to drag women off to the altar at a day's notice.'

She slid away from him, evaded his lunging grasp and quickly wrapped a housecoat around her tingling body.

'Where do you think you're going?' he demanded.

'To get some breakfast. And if you want any you'd better get dressed. I don't entertain naked men in my kitchen.'

She heard him singing in the shower as she drew various items from the refrigerator. Her mouth curved into a happy smile and she found it quite impossible to regret anything that had happened. She had bacon and eggs sizzling in a pan when Patrick suddenly wrapped his arms around her waist and nuzzled the curve of her throat. The image of Paul and Helen flashed through her mind. It seemed incredible that it had only been yesterday when envy had driven her away from their casual intimacy. Now she breathed in the tangy scent of Patrick's after-shave lotion and shivered with pleasure as his hands moved to cup her breasts possessively.

'Stop it! I'm cooking!'

'Mmmmh! Smells good too,' he murmured, completely ignoring her weak protest.

'Patrick, the bacon will burn. There's orange juice on the counter.'

He laughed and let her go. She quickly readjusted her housecoat, flushing in sudden embarrassment. He watched her with an amused gleam in his eye.

'I think married life is going to suit me. Have you any idea how sexy you look, barefoot and dishevelled?'

'You can start being domestic by passing the plates over,' she answered drily.

'In fact I've got it all figured out. You've got a current passport, haven't you?'

'Yes.' She threw him a questioning glance in between forking out the bacon.

'Well then, it's simple. We'll fly to California and get married there.'

She frowned. 'A month's not exactly a long engagement.'

'Who wants engagements?'

'It is the customary procedure.' She lifted out the eggs and handed him a plate. 'Pick up some cutlery and I'll bring in the toast.'

When they were settled at the table Patrick continued his argument. 'Engagements are only for people who need time to make plans. We have no financial problems, two homes to choose from, no one to consider except ourselves. There's absolutely no reason for waiting.'

'Engagements are also for making sure that the couple know what they are doing.'

He looked up guardedly. 'I know what I'm doing. Don't you?'

'I hope so,' she sighed and then gave him a quick smile. 'I get the strong impression that you're bulldozing me. If I'm not careful I'll end up flattened, rolled into a bundle, hoisted on your back and carried off willy-nilly.'

'Well, you needn't think I'll go anywhere without you,' he grinned.

'I can't just drop everything and run off to California with you.'

'Why not?'

'Engagements are also for meeting families, Patrick. You haven't forgotten I have a family, have you?'

Again there was that slight wariness clouding his eyes. 'You're an adult, Ruth. It's your decision, not your family's.'

'I couldn't just leave them. I wouldn't upset them like that. You'll have to meet my parents.'

He frowned. 'There's plenty of time for that after we're married.'

She shook her head, refusing to budge. 'Mum and Dad have been wonderful to me. It will worry them enough to think we're acting hastily.'

'All the more reason to present them with an accomplished fact.'

'No. It would hurt them.'

They had reached an impasse and it was obvious that Ruth would not back down. Patrick hesitated and then asked, 'What if they show disapproval?'

'I would naturally prefer them to like you, but as you pointed out, it's my decision,' she answered slowly.

'If it means so much to you I'll meet them,' he said decisively. 'I'll do my utmost to present a favourable image as a prospective son-in-law,' he added with a sardonic curve to his lips.

'Don't try too hard,' she warned. 'My father is a very astute man.'

'Good God! You don't really mean I'm to be subjected to inspection?'

'I'm afraid so,' she grinned, but he was not amused.

'I'll meet them because you want me to, but not until the day before we fly out. I'm not going to allow anything to come between us.'

'They only want me to be happy, Patrick,' she said with softly pleading eyes.

'So do I,' he assured her seriously. 'Your parents are bound to have preconceived ideas about me. I won't be put in the false position of apologising for my life. I would have preferred to wait until after we're married, let them see that you're happy with me, but since you insist, I'll meet them as a matter of courtesy.'

She could understand his point of view, but it saddened her to think of her parents' disappointment. Her mother would certainly be upset at missing out on a wedding.

'Patrick . . .' she began tentatively.

'No. We'll do it my way, Ruth. See it as humouring me if you like. After we're married, I'll humour you.'

He spoke lightly, but there was fixed purpose behind his words. He reached over for her left hand and drew off John's rings. 'They don't belong there any more. I'll put my ring on that finger tomorrow. We'll go to Sydney and fix your visa, book a flight, make all arrangements necessary.'

'You don't believe in wasting time,' she observed wryly.

'Not when it's so important to me.'

There was a glimmer of vulnerability in his eyes that prompted Ruth to accept his plans without further objection. Everything he said was true, anyway. With a sense of casting her lot completely with him, she nodded.

'All right. We'll do it your way.'

He squeezed her hand and smiled, his face showing a gamut of emotion from relief to triumph. 'You won't regret it, Ruth,' he declared with confidence.

The assurance was no empty one. Patrick gave her no time to entertain any regrets. He filled the hours with laughter and a wild gaiety that bubbled like champagne in her blood. Then there were moments of loving tenderness which were all the more poignant in their contrast. Ruth glowed with happiness.

The next day they went back to Sydney, where Patrick immediately hustled people into organising Ruth's visa. The flight to California was not so easy. January 2nd was the first available booking unless they were willing to stand by for a cancellation. Ruth steadfastly refused that option. With a definite date they could plan their moves.

'What about your Hong Kong trip?' she asked, suddenly recalling Patrick's itinerary.

'It can wait.'

'Haven't you any commitments here? You said you planned on staying until after New Year.'

'Only because the Hindleys pressed me to stay for their New Year's Eve party. I enjoyed the Aussie crowd at Cannes, and Scott said they'd all be at his party, so I accepted.'

'Then you can still go.'

'We can,' he emphasised. 'But only if you'd like to, Ruth. I don't really care now.'

'Maybe we should go,' she suggested thoughtfully. 'I know so little about your kind of life, the people you mix with.'

'As you like,' he shrugged. 'We can drive up and see your parents on New Year's Day, and then collect whatever things you want to take with you.'

'I'll need more time than that, Patrick. Apart from packing up there are notes I need to sort through for my next book.'

He thought for a minute and then said, 'How about Friday? I had a professor lined up to give some background information I wanted. You could go home and organise things on Friday and I can keep my appointment with him.' He suddenly laughed. 'Can't you see us, Ruth? Both chewing our pens over words which won't come? You'll love my house in California. It overlooks the ocean and is completely private. You won't even have to think of meals when you're writing. There's a housekeeper who obliges.'

'Do you really need a wife, Patrick?' she teased.

'I need you, Ruth Devlin, so don't think you can get out of it. Come on. A ring is the next item on the agenda.'

He chose a beautiful, royal blue sapphire, surrounded by diamonds, and then bought two matching wedding rings. It surprised Ruth that he should want to wear one, but secretly she was pleased. It was yet another sign that Patrick was completely sincere in his sentiments. He had given her no reason to doubt it, but occasionally it flitted through her mind that everything was unreal, as if her feet were way off the ground, and sooner or later she would land with a thud. But the dream did not falter. The next two days passed as happily as Ruth could wish. They took a harbour cruise, lay on Bondi Beach, did a host of simple things, made magical by their pleasure in each other.

Patrick did not like the separation on Friday but reluctantly let her go. For a while Ruth drove along automatically, still bemused on his passionate insistence that she waste no time in getting back to him. Then as the kilometres passed, her mind turned to what had to be done. The thought of her parents' reaction disturbed her. As she approached Jirrong, the impulse to prepare them become stronger. It was unfair to leave them ignorant of her plans until the last moment. If she told them now, they would have time to adjust to the idea before meeting Patrick on Sunday. She wanted their approval at that meeting, wanted them to accept Patrick warmly. It would be very hard to go away if they were shocked and unhappy.

Ruth turned into her parents' street. As she braked to a halt a ginger cat streaked across the road. Tuffy followed in hot pursuit. The cat leapt onto a garden wall, then turned and arched its back, hissing defiantly at the little Australian terrier. Tuffy yelped excitedly at having cornered the enemy but carefully kept her distance.

'Coward!' Ruth called out laughingly as she alighted from the station-wagon.

'Ruth!' Her mother suddenly rose from behind some shrubbery.

'Hello, Mum. Doing some gardening?'

'Weeding!' Joyce held up her soiled hands and grimaced. 'I'm glad you called. I've been trying to ring you but you never seem to be at home.' She glanced across the street to where Tuffy was still menacing the cat. 'Leave old Ginger alone, Tuffy. We're going inside.'

Relieved to have an excuse to retreat with honour, the dog trotted back obediently and wagged its tail, obviously expecting praise. Ruth scooped her up and followed her mother inside.

'Your father's mowing the back lawn, but I'm sure he'll be only too happy to leave it for a cup of tea. Let him know you're here, Ruth, while I clean up.'

Her father was pleased to see her. 'Thank God!' he declared, switching off the mower and wiping his brow. 'Why your mother insists that the grass be no higher than half an inch, I'll never know. It's totally against nature. How are you, Ruth? You look particularly glowing this morning. Everything okay again?'

'What do you mean, again?' she grinned at him.

'Oh, you know. I guess Christmas Day is still hard for you.'

'Not any more, Dad. I've got some news for you. Come on in. I can't stay long.'

Ruth wondered how Patrick would react to having cups of tea pushed upon him and the thought amused her as Joyce Devlin bustled around in the kitchen.

'I wanted to ask you in for lunch on New Year's Day,' her mother remarked warmly. 'I didn't like the thought of your being alone. I know you get depressed this time of year.'

'Well, what's the good news?' her father interrupted as he emerged from the laundry. 'I bet you've sold a million copies of your new book already.'

'No!' Ruth laughed. She put Tuffy down on the

floor to cover the slight flush of embarrassment which coloured her cheeks. 'Actually, I'm getting married.'

The stunned expressions on their faces made her feel even more embarrassed. 'I think you'd both better sit down. I'll bring in the tea, Mum.'

'No, it's all right, Ruth,' her mother fluttered. 'It's just such a surprise. You didn't tell us there was anyone. You go and sit down with your father. I'll only be a minute and you can tell us all about it.'

'Married?' her father muttered quizzically as he dropped into a chair.

She nodded, her eyes dancing at him.

'You're happy?'

It was more of a statement than a question but Ruth answered, 'Yes, very happy.'

'When are we going to meet him?'

'On Sunday, if that's all right with you.'

'Of course it's all right,' Joyce Devlin declared as she came in on the last line. 'Now, for goodness' sake, tell us about him. I never imagined you were serious about anyone. Not a word from you, Ruth.'

There was a hurt note in her voice and Ruth chose her words carefully. 'It's been what you might call a whirlwind courtship, Mum. I didn't think Patrick was serious at first, so there was nothing to tell.'

'Patrick?' her father prompted.

'Patrick Hagan, Dad. You both saw him on the television show.'

Again there was a stunned silence, but of different quality. Horror and disapproval chased across her father's face before he schooled his expression to impassivity. It was her mother who spoke first, her voice quivering.

'That Patrick Hagan, Ruth?'

'Yes,' she sighed, her heart sinking like a stone at their totally negative reaction.

'But . . .' Joyce hesitated, at a loss for words. 'He's . . . he's very attractive,' she finished limply.

'How long have you known him, Ruth?' her father asked pointedly.

'Only since the show, Dad. I know it must seem rather hasty to you . . .'

'Hasty! My God! It's only been two weeks!' he shook his head incredulously. 'Doesn't it seem rather hasty to you? I don't know the man, but two weeks appears rather hasty to me.' His concern was natural under the circumstances, but it grated on Ruth. 'I know him, Dad. We're flying to California on Monday and getting married on Tuesday,' she said in one rushed breath, compelled to get it over with. 'I want you and Mum to meet him on Sunday before we go.'

As Martin Devlin digested this information he became more tight-lipped, and Ruth was dismayed to see tears well up in her mother's eyes. Impulsively she reached over and squeezed her hand.

'Come on, Mum. You've been wanting me to get married. You should be happy for me,' she pleaded softly.

'I'm sorry, Ruth,' her mother replied shakily. 'It just feels as though I'm losing you, and I won't even be at your wedding.'

'You won't be losing me, Mum. We'll be back often. I promise you.'

'Yes, dear, if you say so. Don't mind me. I have to get a hanky.'

She blundered off towards her bedroom, too upset to see straight. Tuffy made it more difficult, prancing around her feet as if sensing something wrong. Ruth looked despairingly at her father, but there was no softening on his face.

'Dad, I've got to do what's right for me. I know it's not what you expected. I know it's come as a shock to you. Please try to accept it. I'm happy with him. I want to marry him. It's as simple as that.'

'Is it, Ruth? Do you really believe he loves you?' he said heavily.

'Yes, I do.'

'You said nothing about him at Christmas.'

'I thought then that he only wanted me.'

'Couldn't it be that he only wants you now?' he asked sharply.

She looked at him straight in the eye, determined that he should understand and no longer question. 'No. I've been with him since Christmas night, Dad. He doesn't have to marry me. He wants to marry me.'

He covered his face with one hand and his sigh was almost a groan. Ruth sighed also as she stood up.

'Patrick was right. I shouldn't have told you. I'm going out home to pack. I'll drop any perishable food in to Mum on my way back to Sydney.' Her tone was stilted.

Her father did not reply. She stood stiffly, strode out of the house and almost ran up to the station-wagon. All the way to Tergola she felt choked with emotion and once inside her house she broke down and cried, too distressed even to think of packing. Common sense told her that she had been foolish to expect any other reaction from her parents. Her relationship with Patrick had to seem wrong to them. Patrick was an alien, from a different world altogether, and the speed with which he was sweeping her towards marriage was too unconventional. Ruth wondered at her own complacence, but then re-accepted Patrick's reasoning. There was no point in waiting. The commitment had been made. She should have been more tactful in announcing her intentions to her parents, taken it more slowly, explained more.

There was a sharp ring on the doorbell, and Ruth hastily wiped the tear-stains from her cheeks and went to answer it. Joyce Devlin's anxious face looked back at her.

'Oh dear! Look at you, and you looked so happy this morning.' Her mother threw her arms around Ruth in a loving hug and then held her away to inspect her again. 'Now you put that smile back on your face. We've come to help you pack. Martin's just gone to the supermarket to get some boxes for you.'

Ruth fought back the tears and gave a watery smile. 'Thanks, Mum.'

Joyce Devlin slipped her arm around Ruth's waist, drawing her inside. 'I'm sorry, dear. I was being a selfish old woman, and here you've met a man you can love and be happy with. Now you tell me all about him. I just want to listen.'

'Oh Mum, I do love you,' Ruth whispered, kissing her affectionately.

'But you love him better, which is as it should be,' her mother nodded. 'Now, let's get to work.'

They started in the bedroom, her mother cleaning enthusiastically while Ruth sorted through her clothes. Her father arrived with boxes, gave his daughter a rueful greeting and set about putting all the garden paraphernalia in storage under the house. By the time they sat down to a makeshift lunch most of the work had been done. Her father sat munching his sandwiches with brooding intentness. Ruth was aware that he was almost bursting with disapproval but felt there was nothing she could say to improve the situation. Finally he lit his pipe and cleared his throat.

'Ruth, you know we only want your happiness,' he began tentatively and got a warning look from his wife. 'Joyce, I can't sit back and say nothing,' he protested.

'No. You can say lots of things, but I won't have Ruth going away upset, Martin.'

'Well, dammit! I don't want her coming home upset!' he snapped and then quickly recovered his temper, struggling to compose his expression into that of a reasonable man. 'I only wanted to ask you to wait a while, be sure he's the right man for you. I know he's handsome and glamorous and very worldly-wise and God knows what else, but it's never wise to act in haste, Ruth, not in such a serious step as marriage.'

'We're both very sure, Dad,' she said softly, wanting to erase the concern from his eyes.

He frowned, one hand ruffling his hair in agitation. 'He didn't seem to be the type of man who would attract you, Ruth.'

'There's much more to Patrick than meets the eye. Don't prejudge him, Dad. Wait until you meet him.'

'Ah yes,' he sighed. 'Forgive me, Ruth, but I must ask you if you really believe you can be happy, racketing around the world in an endless pursuit of excitement?'

'I don't think we'll do that.'

'You think Patrick Hagan will be content with just you?'

'Martin!'

The reproof irritated him and his temper flared again. 'Joyce, he's not exactly a spring chicken and he hasn't been able to form a stable relationship so far in his long and varied life. Why should he change for Ruth?' he declaimed hotly.

'Because Ruth is special, that's why, and he has the good sense to know it,' Joyce answered calmly.

Ruth smiled at her mother, gratified by her championship of Patrick. Martin threw up his hands in disgust.

'Is it so unreasonable to ask them to wait a while? Why do they have to race off to California? Why can't they get married here? Why isn't Patrick Hagan with you today?' he demanded in growing exasperation.

'He had an appointment to see a professor. You'll see him on Sunday. As for the rest, Patrick refuses to wait and that's why we're going to California. And, Dad,' she added meaningly, 'that's exactly what we're going to do. So please try to accept it before Sunday.'

'It's madness, Ruth, and you know it,' he said,

drawing his brows together in a tired line. 'I just hope to God you'll be happy with him.'

'Wait and see,' she said confidently.

He was clearly too troubled to take her word. 'One thing, Ruth. If you have any doubts, any doubts at all before your marriage takes place, don't feel obliged to go on with it just because . . . well, because . . .'

She placed a reassuring hand on his arm. 'Don't worry, Dad. Honestly, I do know what I'm doing.'

He nodded and suddenly noticed the sapphire ring on her finger. He drew her hand down and examined it before giving her a wry smile. 'Well, it looks as though he loves you. I'll look forward to meeting him on Sunday.'

'Thanks, Dad.'

His resignation had been reluctant, but the atmosphere eased considerably. The rest of the packing was finished quickly. Ruth emptied the contents of the refrigerator into a carton and handed it to her father. She thanked her parents for their help and having given them her promise to be in good time for Sunday lunch, she kissed them goodbye and waved them off. A lump rose in her throat as she turned back to the house. Her father had suddenly looked old as he had stooped to get into his car, and despite her mother's brave attempt to smooth over the situation, there had been a forlorn expression in her eyes. It seemed wrong that her happiness should be causing them pain.

Ruth wandered through each room of her house, re-checking everything for the last time. She felt a strange disquiet, knowing she was turning her back on all that was familiar to her. The photograph album still lay on the sideboard. She slipped it into a drawer, rejecting the temptation to look through it once more. That life was over and a new life was beginning. She passed the luggage stacked in the hall, locked the front door and walked out to the station-wagon without looking back.

'What took you so long?' Patrick demanded as soon as she walked into the hotel suite. 'I was beginning to worry about you. I shouldn't have let you out of my sight.' He swung the light suitcase she had brought out of her hand and onto a chair. Then wrapping her in iron-tight arms, he muttered into her hair, 'Don't do this to me again, Ruth.'

She was bewildered by his vehemence but felt too drained emotionally to question it. 'You knew where I was, Patrick,' she sighed tiredly.

'God almighty! I was imagining all sorts of things. I shouldn't have let you go on your own.'

She rested her head on his shoulder, content to feel the strength of his body. 'No, it was better that I did,' she murmured.

Abruptly he drew back from her, his hands gripping her upper arms. 'What do you mean by that? What's been going on, Ruth?'

She looked up into darkly suspicious eyes and shivered. 'What's the matter with you, Patrick? You're hurting me.'

He immediately loosened his hold and rubbed her arms. 'I'm sorry, darling.' There was a tautness about his features and the smile he gave her seemed forced. 'Forgive me?'

She nodded and turned away, troubled by the

tension he was generating. 'Let's sit down and have a drink. I want to talk to you.' She slipped her shoes off and collapsed into the nearest armchair. 'I feel exhausted.'

'What did you do to make you so tired?' he asked casually as he mixed the drinks.

She waited until he was sitting down before answering. 'I saw Mum and Dad.'

For a moment anger flashed into his eyes but he spoke in a flat, controlled voice. 'I thought we agreed to leave that until Sunday.'

She shook her head sadly. 'That wouldn't have worked.'

'They've upset you.'

'They're worried, that's all.'

'They tried to talk you out of it.'

'Not exactly. They'd like us to wait, get married here,' she explained calmly.

'And you? What did you say?'

She frowned, disliking the harsh tone of his voice. 'I said our plans had been made and they wouldn't be changed.'

He let out a long, shuddering breath, but before he could gather himself for any comment, she added quickly, 'That's what I want to talk to you about.'

'No!' The word exploded from him, startling her. 'We are not changing any plans. I figured you'd gone to see them when you were so late getting back here. I've been going through hell, wondering how you'd cope with their opposition. I know all about that kind of emotional blackmail and I won't tolerate it, Ruth.'

'Patrick, listen to me,' she pleaded. 'My parents

wouldn't dream of using emotional blackmail to stop me doing what I wanted.' She saw the hard disbelief in his eyes and tried again. 'Look, I know you've never had a real family and I realise you don't understand, but I love my parents and I hurt them today. It would have been even more hurtful if I'd left it until Sunday. They're old. I didn't realise how old.'

'That's right!' he cut in bluntly. 'They've had their lives, are still having their life together. We have our life to live, Ruth, and we're not waiting on anyone or anything.'

She bowed her head, knowing he was both right and wrong. 'I only wanted you to promise me that we'd come back soon and visit them.'

'Is that all?' The relief in his voice was almost tangible. He pulled Ruth onto her feet, his eyes glittering down at her. 'I thought I'd have to fight them.' Then he laughed and lifted her into his arms. 'I'd fight the whole damned world for you. Give me a month, no, two months, and then we'll come back and visit your parents. Will that do?'

She linked her arms around his neck and smiled. 'Can we tell them that on Sunday?'

'Yes, tell them by all means, if it makes you happy.' He laid her gently on the bed and stretched out beside her. His hand stroked the curve of her cheek and he added huskily, 'So long as you're mine.'

Then slowly and effectively he erased every thought from Ruth's mind, leaving only a burning need for his love.

CHAPTER EIGHT

'WEAR the blue dress,' Patrick advised as Ruth looked uncertainly at her clothes.

'Are you sure? I don't want to look out of place.'

Her dubious glance took in his rather swash-buckling outfit; form-fitting black slacks and a white satin shirt, half opened to reveal the virile tanned chest. He looked blatantly sexy in a lithe vital way and it undermined Ruth's confidence. She was used to men in more conservative dress, had always suspected that only narcissistic extroverts wore such clothes. But Patrick was an extrovert, she reminded herself, and he was well aware of physical attraction, deliberately using it when it suited him. They were uncomfortable thoughts as she slipped the blue dress from its hanger and put it on.

'I'll zip you up,' Patrick offered, taking the opportunity to kiss the nape of her neck.

Ruth's skin prickled at the light sensuality of his touch. He looked over her shoulder at her reflection and gave a wolfish grin.

'I love you in that dress. Hold still for a minute.' His arms came around her and then he was hanging a magnificent blue opal pendant around her neck.

'Oh, Patrick!' Ruth gasped. 'It's beautiful!'

Their eyes met in the mirror, hers glowing with pleasure, his warm with satisfaction.

'As soon as I saw it I had to buy it for you. It's

perfect for that dress and perfect for you. Cool Ruth with hidden fire,' he teased.

'Not so hidden,' she said huskily, turning in his arms. 'Thank you.'

Their kiss stirred the fires of passion between them, and Ruth broke away with a selfconscious laugh.

'I'll never be ready at this rate.'

Patrick's eyes glinted possessively. 'You look ready now.'

'Oh no, I'm not. I'll need some make-up to compete with all those she-wolves who'll be casting their eyes over you.'

'I'll only see a girl in blue.'

'You'd better. I have a possessive streak of my own, you know.'

He laughed delightedly, running a provocative finger over her back as she attempted to brush on some eye-shadow.

'You're making it impossible,' she accused.

'Ruth?' His eyes were suddenly serious.

'Mmm?'

'We'll keep our plans private tonight. I don't want a circus, and it'd be a three-ring, all-star circus if that crowd learned we were getting married.'

She gave him a wry smile. 'You mean if they learned that you were getting married.'

He shrugged and returned her smile. 'In fact, I'm not sure it's a good idea to go at all. I'd rather have you to myself.'

'What are you afraid of, Patrick?' she asked perceptively.

His gaze held hers for a moment, oddly speculative. Then he shook his head. 'Nothing. Are you ready now?'

'Yes.'

Patrick drove her station-wagon rather than rely on taxis. New Year's Eve made cabs a rare commodity. It was only a short drive, and he amused Ruth with comments about some of the expected guests. She recognised the names of several film and television personalities and was curious to meet them. She hoped that tonight's party would provide her with an insight into the kind of world she would be sharing with Patrick.

They drew up outside an impressive Spanish-style house set in extensive gardens. Scott Hindley's home represented wealth on an unfamiliar scale, and it was with some trepidation that Ruth accompanied Patrick to the front door. Their host was effusive in his welcome, and it was not until his wife turned back from greeting earlier visitors that Ruth's confidence plummeted further.

Lissa Hindley was the glamorous blonde who had been with Patrick at the television studio. Her eyes now lighted on him warmly but frosted over quickly when he introduced Ruth. For a split second there was naked hostility in that green gaze before she spoke with saccharine condescension.

'Of course. You're the young schoolteacher who writes books. It was very sweet of you to bring Miss Devlin along, darling.'

'Quite frankly, Lissa, I would not have come without her,' Patrick replied smoothly, smiling down at Ruth.

It was a soft snub, making his position quite clear,

and Patrick did not bother to watch it hit its mark. Ruth saw Lissa Hindley's eyes narrow and she wondered if her hostess had entertained any fanciful designs on Patrick and if he had encouraged them. She squashed the thought as soon as it rose, determined not to be rattled by anything.

She and Patrick were soon swept up in a whirl of introductions and airy chatter. The first couple of hours passed quickly, Patrick ensuring her inclusion in any conversation and Ruth growing in confidence as she fitted names to faces. They eventually settled into a group of people gathered on the patio. Having answered the few questions directed at her, Ruth sat back, content to listen to the talk flowing around her.

Gossip about various celebrities was exchanged and the prevailing element of cynical bitchiness caused her some disquiet, particularly as Patrick was obviously enjoying it. The conversation was sparkling but laced too liberally with sexual double-meanings, suggesting an unhealthy absorption in physical games. As she perceived that the wit was subtly cruel and the friendliness suspiciously brittle, she began pondering if such company would ever hold any real pleasure for her.

'Patrick, you old son of a gun!' The booming voice stopped the conversation and everyone turned to see Rex Thornton bearing down on them, a broad grin all over his handsome face. 'Glad to see you looking fit and virile, though how the hell you do it I don't know.' He shook Patrick's hand, greeted the others in his boisterous manner and eyed Ruth with interest.

'Uh-uh,' Patrick shook his head warningly. 'She's

mine. Rex Thornton, Ruth, and don't let him an inch closer.'

'Ruth?' His eyebrows shot up in the characteristic gesture Ruth had seen in several films. He was one of Australia's most popular actors.

'Devlin,' she supplied with a smile.

'I might just contest your claim, old son,' he declared provocatively and dropped into a nearby chair.

'You'd be straining a friendship,' Patrick retorted drily.

'Friendship he calls it! My God! They had to load me into the plane after that last party at Cannes, and I didn't become conscious until somewhere over the Pacific.'

Patrick began to laugh and Rex became more eloquent.

'You leader of sin! Warn me off, would you? After snaffling all the nubile women from under my nose and encouraging me to a drunken orgy, you have the unmitigated gall to warn me off. I tell you, Ruth, I am a lamb of innocence compared to him.'

This last claim gave rise to hoots of derisive laughter from everyone. Ruth laughed also but she did not feel amused. Scott Hindley suddenly appeared and beckoned Patrick aside. He moved reluctantly, but after a few words with his host he came back to Ruth, looking apologetic.

'There are a few things Scott wants to discuss about my book. Will you be all right here for a while, or would you prefer to come with me?'

'Go ahead. I'll be all right here,' she assured him. No sooner was Patrick out of sight than Rex

Thornton took the vacated chair. 'Tell me about yourself,' he demanded flirtatiously.

'Forget it, Rex. I'm his,' she grinned, mocking his attempt to interest her.

'Damn, damn damn! A constant woman! What's he got that I haven't?'

'I don't know. Why don't you tell me about yourself, and I might work it out.'

He accepted the invitation with relish and regaled her with interesting snatches of his life. He was an amusing raconteur, but Ruth grew restive as time passed and Patrick's absence became more prolonged. She finally decided to look for him.

'Excuse me, please, Rex. I think I'll find the powder room.'

'A word of truth, dear girl,' he murmured, and there was a hint of malice in his eyes. 'You might be constant, but he isn't. Seek and ye shall find.'

Ruth flushed and turned away, irritated by the insinuation. Rex Thornton was beating his own drum, but an uncertain flutter crept into her pulse. She felt as much an alien in Patrick's world as he probably would in hers. There was no sign of Patrick amongst the milling guests, but Scott Hindley was in evidence, laughing with a group of people. A knot of apprehension twisted her stomach and she made her way to the powder room, telling herself firmly that Patrick's absence was completely innocent.

She freshened up her wilting make-up, feeling reluctant to rejoin the party. She forced herself to walk out into the hallway and then hesitated, wishing she had not come here tonight. Curt with exasperation, Patrick's voice sounded clearly over the hubbub of noise. She glanced around in surprise, realising it had come from a room off the hallway. The door was ajar and without thinking she pushed it open, an eager smile on her lips.

Ruth fled without making a sound. She mingled with the crowd, unconscious of her surroundings until a drink waiter bumped into her. She took a drink from his tray and gulped it down quickly, hoping the punch of alcohol would shock her mind into activity. The image of Lissa Hindley in Patrick's arms only sharpened more painfully. It had not been a casual embrace. Patrick's hands had stood out starkly, one moving slowly over the naked back, the other curving intimately on a rounded hip. Lissa Hindley had been clinging to him passionately and there was no innocence at all in the movement of their mouths. Ruth could not think what to do. Her heart was pounding like a jackhammer and she wandered aimlessly towards the patio.

'Find him?'

She stared blankly at Rex Thornton, completely disoriented.

'No? Well his loss is my gain. Come and dance, my lovely.'

He swept Ruth off to where several couples were gyrating to a rock beat. She allowed the rhythm to wash into her body, automatically following Rex's movements. It was something to do until she could think.

'It's no use hitching yourself to him, you know.'

The expression startled her and she looked up at Rex warily.

'Patrick's only passing through. Now, I'm a much better bet. This is my home town.'

He was only flirting. 'I'm not hunting,' Ruth stated flatly.

He caught her to him and deliberately slowed their dancing to a few sensuous movements. 'Are you quite sure? We could make beautiful music together.'

She wrinkled her nose at him in disgust. 'Can't you do better than that line, Rex? It's straight out of a B-movie.'

He rolled his eyes, seeking inspiration. 'How about "Come with me to the Casbah"?' The invitation was delivered with low melodrama and much movement of eyebrows as he twirled her around and bent her over his arm.

'That's enough, Rex. Beat it!' Patrick's voice cracked like a whip, slicing through the nonsense.

'Pardon me, old son,' Rex intoned solemnly, letting Ruth go and salaaming in mock obeisance.

Patrick ignored him, enfolding Ruth in his arms and pressing her to him in suffocating closeness. 'I don't want you in anyone's arms but mine, Ruth.'

Hysteria bubbled up in her throat, but she choked it back. The ache in her heart became a full-blooded pain at this further example of Patrick's hypocrisy.

'Godammit! Couldn't you see what type he is?' he suddenly demanded, his body tense with anger as they moved to the music.

'I thought you had a lot in common,' she retorted icily.

He glanced down at her still, pale face and sighed.

'I'm sorry. I'm being stupid, aren't I? To tell you the truth I've never felt jealous before.'

'Used to sharing your women, Patrick,' she jibed at him.

He stopped dancing and looked at her more sharply. 'What's Rex been telling you?'

'The truth, I imagine.'

He made a wry grimace. 'Yes, I suppose it was.' His hand came up and lightly caressed her cheek. 'That's in the past, Ruth.'

'Is it? I don't want to dance any more, Patrick. I'd like a long, very alcoholic drink.'

She turned away from him and he caught her arm, stopping her. 'What's the matter, Ruth?'

'You had no right to act the jealous lover.'

He frowned at the bitterness in her voice. 'I have apologised,' he said softly.

'What did you expect me to do while you were about your business? Crouch in a corner?'

'Of course not.'

'Is that what you expected of our marriage? Have me as background music while you play your own fiddle?'

'Ruth!' He was taken aback by her vehemence, puzzled concern in his eyes. 'How can you say that?'

She swallowed the words which had almost tripped off her tongue. This was not the place for those words. She dropped a mask of composure over her feelings and replied evasively. 'I really do need a drink.'

'Okay,' he nodded, still disquieted by her taut manner.

He was leading her inside when they were waylaid

by the other woman Ruth remembered from the television show.

'Patrick! There you are! Mmm, you do look rakish tonight,' she crooned, sliding her hand into the opening of his shirt.

'And you, my pet, have had one drink too many,' he drawled, removing her hand.

She pouted provocatively. 'Aren't you going to give me a kiss for New Year?'

'Not until the bell tolls. I'll see you later.'

The blithe promise set Ruth's teeth on edge. She could not tolerate this scene any longer. She owed no courtesy to anyone here and to stay would only prolong the agony.

'I want to go, Patrick.'

'Now?'

'Now.'

His first surprise quickly deepened to worried concern. 'Tell me what's wrong, Ruth.'

'You can either take me back to the hotel or give me the keys to the wagon. I'm going now,' she stated coldly.

He looked at her determined face, then steered her outside without a word to anyone. They drove back to the hotel in a tense silence. Patrick waited until the door of the suite closed behind them before challenging her. His arms reached out, but she eluded his grasp and headed straight for the cupboard which stored their suitcases.

'What the hell's going on?' he demanded angrily as she lifted out her cases.

'I'm going home, back where I belong. I'm not marrying you, Patrick.'

He strode across the room and turned her to face him. 'Is it too much to ask why?' he grated out.

She met his gaze steadily, refusing to flinch. 'No. The answer's very simple. I don't want to share your life.'

He sucked in his breath and let it out slowly, straining to keep control of barely leashed emotions. 'What happened to change your mind?'

'You mean what removed the scales from my eyes so that I could see where I was heading?' she threw at him bitterly.

'An explanation would be helpful,' he retorted with equal bitterness.

'That was your life back there, Patrick. Why don't you go back to it?'

'You were the one who wanted to go to that damned party. As far as I was concerned, it was meaningless.'

'You're so right!' she flared back at him. 'Meaningless is exactly the word! And you enjoyed every meaningless minute of it, all the meaningless chatter, the sexual innuendos, the glib flattery, even the meaningless kisses. Or weren't they so meaningless, Patrick?'

His eyes narrowed and Ruth felt a savage satisfaction as the shaft sank home. She swept her dresses into a suitcase, cramming them in carelessly. As she opened a drawer, Patrick slammed it shut.

'You're not going anywhere. We'll talk this out and get it straight.' He dragged her over to a chair and sat her down. 'Stay there! I'll get you that long, alcoholic drink you wanted.'

Ruth suddenly found she was trembling and realised it was a delayed reaction to shock. She accepted the drink without protest but firmly held onto her resolve to go as soon as she felt steadier.

'I presume you're not talking about kisses of greeting, so that leaves Lissa Hindley,' he stated grimly.

Ruth disdained to answer. She sipped the drink he had handed her, waiting for the warm tingle of alcohol to invade her veins.

'It was not at my invitation, Ruth. I'd finished with Scott and was about to rejoin you when Lissa angled me into that room. She wanted to play and I declined as gracefully as I could.'

'Very gracefully,' Ruth bit out sarcastically.

'What would you expect me to do? Slap her face? I told her it wasn't on. That kiss was a last attempt to change my mind. I didn't change it. I didn't want to change it.'

'But you gave it a damned good test. Nothing half-hearted about that goodbye. Passed off with honours, I'd say,' she spat at him, contempt coating every word. 'And I suppose what's-her-name, Kate, would've got the same treatment at a convenient moment. And any other woman who took a fancy to you. You wouldn't slap any of them down, would you, Patrick?'

'I think you've got things a bit out of perspective, Ruth,' he said tersely. 'After all, it was a New Year's Eve party.'

'Licence for lechery?' she mocked him viciously.

'Don't start dramatising something that means nothing.' His hand sliced the air with angry emphasis. 'Nothing! You're the only woman I want, Ruth.'

'Well, I don't want you.'

The words were delivered with icy disdain, her eyes stabbing the rejection home. He paled, the tanned face becoming quite sallow.

'You don't mean that. You're upset.'

'Several shades deeper than you were when you found me dancing with Rex Thornton.' Her voice dripped with venom. 'The bottom had just fallen out of my world and Rex found me standing alone like a puppet without a string. He simply swept me off to dance. I could barely go through the motions. You came in fighting jealous, hot from another woman's arms. You think I'll live with that double standard? Never!'

He flinched, recognising the deadliness of the accusation. 'Let me explain,' he said quickly. 'About Lissa . . .'

'I don't want to hear.'

'Be fair, Ruth,' he demanded.

She stared at him stonily but remained seated.

'It was the easiest way to get away from her. If I hadn't bent a little, she would have made a nuisance of herself for the rest of the evening. She's the type.'

'I see. You'd rather offend me than offend her.'

'No, dammit!' he bit out savagely. 'I wanted her out of my hair, the stupid bitch. She was spoiling for a scene, trying to cling onto something that never was. She crawled into my bed one night at Cannes and I made the mistake of not kicking her out. It's past, Ruth, nothing to do with you and me. Can't you see that?'

'No, I can't see that,' she retorted fiercely. 'I can

see a long line of ex-mistresses, or not so ex, all expecting some casual intimacy. You enjoy your powers of attraction. You're a very sexual animal. That's your immediate impact and you play it to the hilt. It repelled me when I first met you and it repels me now.'

'Does it?' he grated out, his mouth a thin, ugly line. Before Ruth could move he had snatched the glass from her hand and pulled her to her feet. She struggled vainly against the strength of his arms. His eyes glittered down at her, burning coals of determination. 'I won't let you go, Ruth.'

Realising it was futile to pit her strength against his, she stood passively, pinned against his body.

'It's no use, Patrick,' she muttered dully. 'You can't hold me forever.'

All the bleakness of disillusion was in her voice. She felt his chest expand as he drew in a deep breath and his arms tightened around her.

'Ruth, I need you,' he breathed out raggedly. 'Don't leave me.'

The plea twisted like a knife in her heart, weakening her resolve. He rubbed his cheek gently against her hair, a desperate longing in the simple action. The stiffness seeped out of her body, and feeling the new pliancy, he lifted one hand away to curve around her chin and tilt her head upwards. His eyes searched hers anxiously.

'I love you, only you,' he insisted softly. 'No one else matters a damn.'

'Only when no one else is around,' she sighed, unable to believe him yet unable to tear herself away.

'Ruth, I swear to you . . .'

'Don't! Actions speak louder than words,' she said with bitter irony.

'So they do,' he agreed tersely and before she could divine his intention, his mouth was on hers, warmly persuasive, passionately intent on arousing a response. She yielded with passive indifference, cold ashes to his fire. And yet, he fanned a reluctant spark. With all the lover's skill at his command he breathed life into those dead ashes, and her traitorous body melted under the furnace of kisses, the practised caress of his hands, the whole sum of his seductive mastery.

'I love you, I love you,' he whispered, the words echoing relentlessly, filling the vast emptiness which had opened at his betrayal of her trust, dazing her into compliance.

She wanted to believe him, needed to believe him, yearned for his love with a desperate hunger. Then suddenly she became aware of his hand, roaming lightly over the naked skin of her back. The sharp image of that hand doing the same to Lissa Hindley burned across her mind. She pushed him away violently.

'You bastard! You cynical bastard!' she panted, zipping up her dress as she backed away from him. His love-making had stripped away the controlled numbness, baring the agony in her heart. An unintelligible sound broke from her throat. Tears welled up in her eyes and spilled over. She swallowed convulsively, needing to release the words which were choking her. 'You thought that would keep me. You thought you only had to use your very practised technique and the poor little, love-starved woman would fall flat on her back.'

'No!'

He reached out for her and she lashed blindly at him, striking a glancing blow to the chin. His head jerked back and she retreated further.

'Keep away from me!'

'For God's sake, Ruth!'

'Don't touch me! If you think I'll marry you for that you're mistaken. You've kept me drugged with your love-making all week, but I won't fall into that trap again. It's what you rely on to keep a woman happy, and you're very good at it, but it's not enough, Patrick, not nearly enough. It's too cheap a commodity.' Contempt shimmered through the tears, stopping him more forcefully than any blow. 'I'll finish packing now and then I'm going. Nothing you can say or do will stop me.'

She ignored him, refusing to recognise his presence as she piled her belongings into the suitcases. The light glinted on her ring as she clicked them shut. Slowly she drew it off, and steeling herself for this last goodbye, her eyes sought Patrick. He sat hunched over, his head in his hands, and for a moment Ruth's determination faltered, her heart pleading for another chance. Then she sealed the agony away, walked over to the coffee-table in front of him and placed the ring next to his untouched drink.

'Don't go, Ruth.'

His head jerked up and the despair in his eyes was heartbreakingly real. The angles of his face seemed harsher, the skin taut and sickly.

'I'm sorry. I must,' she said stiffly.

'You said you loved me.'

The pain in his voice stabbed at her but she kept her purpose steady. 'I loved a dream. I've woken up now, Patrick. I can't live with your reality. Please give me the car keys and let me go.'

He shook his head.

'It won't stop me. It will only inconvenience me.'

He made no response and Ruth heaved a sigh and moved to pick up her suitcases. The opal pendant dangled in front of her eyes as she bent over. Her hands moved instinctively to undo the catch.

'Keep it!' The hoarse cry startled her. She glanced back as a jangle of keys fell at her feet. 'If you're going, then go!' he added savagely.

'I don't want to keep it,' she fired back at him even as her fingers trembled uselessly, clumsy in their haste.

'I have no use for it.' He rose to his feet, menacing in his angry frustration. His hand flew out in fierce dismissal. 'Do you think I want anything to remind me of you? Go on, go! Go back to your safe little world where people don't make mistakes which can't be forgiven.'

He twisted away in violent rejection, his back stiff and unrelenting. For a moment Ruth was stunned by his outburst. Then she picked up the keys and the suitcases and hurried to the door. She glanced back as she opened it, her eyes drawn once more to the man she had scorned. His head was thrown back in a listening attitude, his body ramrod straight and tense.

'You didn't make mistakes, Patrick,' she said

sadly. 'You followed your pattern. It was I who made the mistake. Goodbye.'

Ruth could not drive very far. The tears started flowing, obscuring her vision. Rather than risk an accident she pulled into the side of the road and let the dam burst. Great sobs racked her and she rested her head on the steering-wheel, holding herself tightly to contain the pain in her heaving body. She wept for her dream, mourning its passing in heart-wrenching grief. The tears finally ceased but the pain remained, constricting her chest and throbbing in her head. The drive home was a nightmare. The distance was covered mechanically, Ruth barely grasping at the concentration required to keep her going.

Her home stood waiting for her, a sanctuary where she could find ease for the trauma that had engulfed her. She entered it with deep relief, almost staggering into the bedroom. Her ravaged face stared back at her from the mirror. The opal pendant gleamed at her wickedly, mocking the wreckage of her love. She snatched at it, tearing it off her neck as if it was contaminated and thrusting it away in a drawer, unable to bear the sight of it. In a frenzy she divested herself of the dress Patrick had so admired. Shivering, she curled up in her bed, wrapping the blankets tightly around her, desperately seeking oblivion. It was finished, over, and sleep offered the only escape from her torment.

CHAPTER NINE

SHE was pregnant. Ruth had known even before her doctor had confirmed the fact, but she had not wanted to believe it. She had not wanted to accept that Fate would play such a trick on her. She remembered Patrick's saying he would like to have a family, and depression rolled over her in another destructive wave. She yearned to tell him, have him fly to her, hold her in his arms, tell her once again that he loved her. Then she bitterly reminded herself that a child would no more fit into his world than she would.

Once again she clamped down on emotional weakness. She had been right to reject him. To think of running to him now because she was pregnant was pure self-indulgence. Patrick would not want her anyway. She had flayed him with scorn, virtually called him a whore and turned her back on him. If he had loved her, she had surely trampled that love to death. She was going to have a baby and she would have it on her own.

Her first step was to resign from her teaching job. She explained to her friends on the school staff that she had decided to concentrate on her writing and they accepted her word unquestioningly. She told no one of her pregnancy. Her involvement with Patrick was too hurtful a subject to bring out into the open.

Even with her parents she had refused to discuss her break-up with him. She could not accept their sympathy or comfort because they had never understood her love for him. It had been a difficult duty to continue visiting them. The questions in their eyes made such visits too painful.

As the weeks passed by Ruth stopped seeing friends, was even reluctant to leave the house. She closed in upon herself and the house closed in on her. Patrick haunted it. She not only carried his child, she could not wipe his image from her mind. It was impossible to settle to any writing, and tears were all too ready to fall at any upset. There were six long months to get through before the birth of her baby, and Ruth decided that if she was to do anything constructive she had to leave Tergola, go somewhere else, away from memories.

On Easter Sunday she drove into Jirrong. Her parents' pressing invitation to lunch provided the opportunity to confide in them. She could not keep them in ignorance any longer, now that she was intent on going away. They greeted her with their usual warmth, Tuffy adding her doggy devotion to the welcome. Ruth tried to relax and respond naturally to their conversation, but her inner tension told in stilted replies. Her mother produced the inevitable roast dinner and somehow Ruth managed to do it justice. They were sitting over a cup of tea when she finally screwed up enough courage to speak what was on her mind. Then suddenly her father forestalled her.

'Ruth, it's been almost four months now. Your mother and I understand that you find it painful to talk about what happened last Christmas, but we're both very worried about you.'

'You look so dreadful, dear,' Joyce chimed in anxiously. 'I'm sure you're not looking after yourself. Now that you've given up teaching, won't you come and stay with us for a while? At least until you pick up a bit.'

Their loving concern brought a lump to Ruth's throat and she bit her lips, fighting to hold back the tears which were pricking at her eyes.

'You can do what you like. We won't poke into your privacy, Ruth,' her father added earnestly.

She shook her head. 'I'm going away.' A swift look of alarm darted between her parents and she added, 'I thought I'd go up to the Blue Mountains, a complete change of scenery.'

'Ah, a holiday,' her father sighed in relief. 'Well, maybe that's a good idea.'

'Not exactly a holiday, Dad. I won't be coming back for a while. I'm going to rent a house and live there, probably for the rest of the year.'

'But, Ruth,' her mother frowned, 'it'll be so cold up there with winter coming on.'

'I have to go, Mum.' She sighed, knowing that the moment could not be put off any longer. 'I'm expecting a baby. It's due at the end of September.'

'Oh, my dear,' her mother said sadly. Then as tears spilled from her daughter's eyes she quickly stood up and put her arm comfortingly around Ruth. In the gentle, loving understanding of the gesture, it was not necessary for words to be spoken.

A shudder ran through Ruth as she fought to control her emotion. She clumsily wiped the tears away and took a deep breath. 'I'm sorry, Mum,' she gasped out. 'I didn't want to worry you, but I need your help.'

'Of course, dear,' her mother said tenderly and sent a warning look to her husband, who was sitting in grim silence. 'What can we do? You know you can count on us to help in any way we can.'

Ruth glanced at her father tentatively, then swung her gaze back to her mother. 'I'd be grateful if you'd come and stay with me when the baby's due.'

'Ruth, won't you reconsider and stay here with us? Do you have to go so far away?' she pleaded.

Desperation shaded Ruth's voice as she replied, 'I need to be alone, Mum.'

'Ruth,' her father interrupted in a gruff voice. 'Have you been in touch with Patrick Hagan?'

She shook her head.

'Why not?'

'Now, Martin,' Joyce began reprovingly.

'Dammit, Joyce! He is the father. Ruth loved him enough to . . .'

'Don't, Dad. Please don't go on,' she whispered, lifting pain-filled eyes to him. 'I won't tell Patrick.'

Frustration and anger contorted Martin Devlin's face as he crashed his fist down on the table. 'That selfish, no-good fly-by-night! The least he could have done was look after you so you weren't left . . .'

'Martin, you shut up this instant!'

He glared at his wife who glared fiercely back at him.

'It was my responsibility as well as his,' Ruth inserted quietly, drawing their attention back to herself. 'And the responsibility is completely mine now because I rejected him. That's why I won't tell him, Dad. I wouldn't marry him then when he begged me to and I won't accept anything from him now. So please, let's drop the subject.'

'But you loved him, Ruth,' her mother said faintly.

A spasm of pain tore at Ruth's heart, uncovering the truth which she had tried so hard to ignore. She had loved Patrick. She still loved him. Despite his faults and his cynical life-style, she ached to have him with her—not the Patrick of that last night, but the man he had revealed to her during the days they had spent together. Then the memory of that fateful party injected its poison, shadowing all the rest, and she looked at her mother with all the bleakness of despair.

'Leave it alone, Mum. I'll have my baby and get on with my own life. That's what I've got to do. I'll be leaving next week.'

Her parents finally accepted her decision, although they were clearly worried by it. They fussed over her continually in the following week, reminding her of things she might have forgotten and handing out advice as they helped her pack up. Ruth had not wanted their help, but knew the activity eased their anxiety. She promised to write to them regularly, assured them that she would look after herself sensibly and agreed to rent a house which had a telephone. It was a relief to bid them goodbye and get on her way.

Since it was the off-season Ruth had a good choice of holiday cottages in the Katoomba area. Being the tourist centre of the Blue Mountains it had the most to offer in the way of scenery and conveniences. She finally leased a small house which looked out over rugged cliffs and tree-filled valleys, something totally different from the view at home.

It did not take her long to settle in and establish a regular routine. Knowing she must take care of herself and realising the necessity of self-discipline, she limited herself to five hours' work a day on her book and took long scenic walks for exercise, enjoying the soothing atmosphere of the mountains. There was a timelessness about them which pulled her private problems into proper perspective.

The days quickly became shorter and colder, and Ruth found herself purchasing an electric blanket for the first time, as well as much warmer clothes than she was accustomed to wearing in winter. She stocked up on food, aware that she would become housebound if it snowed. Letters came regularly from her parents and she replied to them conscientiously, easing their fears, assuring them that she paid regular visits to a doctor and she was fine.

One morning she woke up to see a blanket of snow outside, and with the excitement of a child, she quickly dressed and went out, breathing in the sharp, bracing air. With uninhibited pleasure she made snowballs, hurling them at trees and laughing if she hit one. Her laughter triggered the memory of other laughter and slowly she allowed the memories that she had stifled to trickle back into her mind.

They had been so good, those days between Christmas and New Year, scintillating with a very special happiness and warm with the wonderful intimacy of love. Looking back now from the perspective of time and distance, Ruth at last conceded that she had been too hasty in rejecting Patrick. She had judged harshly and had turned her back on a love that might well have overcome their differences if she had been more patient and tolerant.

Patrick had loved her. Those days could not have had their magical quality without love, given and returned. He had loved her, but one week together had not been long enough to alter ingrained attitudes to life. He had declared his kiss with Lissa Hindley meaningless, and now, finally, Ruth believed him. Patrick had played meaningless, sexual games for years, and the habits of a lifetime could not be expected to change overnight.

She remembered the need and despair on his face as she had poured out her contempt. She had been deaf and blind to his pleas, but not dumb. Oh no, not dumb. The deadly words had spilled off her tongue, blistering, cruel, hateful words. Her pride had killed his love for her as surely as if she had plunged a knife into him, and it was a futile exercise to keep twisting the knife in her own heart.

Patrick had made no attempt to see or speak to her again. She remembered his vehement cry that he wanted nothing to remind him of her, and Ruth had no doubt that he had closed the door on that episode in his life. He would have locked it firmly and thrown away the key. She wondered where he was now, if he had found consolation with some other woman. There would always be other women for Patrick in his world of bright lights and fast living.

But other men for her? No. She could not imagine so. She would go on living in her safe little world . . . but not alone. She would have her baby to love. The thought suddenly blossomed with warm pleasure. All this time she had been rejecting it, viewing her pregnancy as a punishment for last year's weakness. Now she hugged her arms across her swollen body and a pure shaft of love was directed at the child growing inside her. Patrick would never come her way again, but she would always have part of him. This child was hers. Her baby.

That morning was a turning-point for Ruth. With a greater sense of purpose in life she finished off her book and posted it to Clive with a covering letter. She had not told him about her pregnancy and she did not tell him now. Her letter instructed him to handle all publishing decisions, that she was on holiday and did not want to be bothered with any unnecessary details. She knew Clive would look after her manuscript with his usual zeal.

With nothing to think about now but the baby, Ruth took pleasure in choosing baby clothes and making the necessary purchases for her confinement. She bought a light carry-cot for immediate purposes, leaving other nursery equipment for when she went home to Tergola.

Although she did not mind what sex her baby was, she found herself thinking of it as a boy. Memories of David's birth flitted through her mind and she hoped this birth would give her as much happiness. The waiting time was almost over and Ruth was impatient for that precious moment when she would at last hold her child in her arms.

Joyce Devlin arrived and spent the time fussing around, making Ruth feel indulgent and irritated in turn, but when the time came she was glad of her mother's presence. Her son came squalling into the world in the evening of the 28th of September and he was laid gently in her arms immediately afterwards. Tears swam into her eyes as she saw the head of tight black curls. She clutched the baby to her convulsively, wishing with all her heart that Patrick had been with her, sharing the birth of their son.

The doctor saw her tears and sent her a reassuring grin. 'He's a perfect child, Miss Devlin. No need to worry about him with those lungs.'

'I know,' she smiled. 'He's beautiful.' A warm rush of maternal love engulfed her as she cradled the baby and she was comforted by his tiny presence.

Ruth called her son Andrew and took delight in feeding and caring for him. Even so she had too much time to think while she was in hospital. Whenever she held Andrew in her arms she was forcibly reminded of Patrick. Martin Devlin had travelled up to join his wife. Each day her parents visited her, bringing comfort and support, but still she suffered bouts of depression. The doctor declared that this was quite natural after giving birth, but Ruth knew its roots went deeper than that.

One day she was still nursing Andrew when her father arrived to sit with her. Her eyes were brimming with tears and she was unable to hide her distress from him. He drew his chair closer to the bedside and squeezed her hand sympathetically.

'What is it, love? Can't you tell your old Dad?' he asked gently, and Ruth could not contain the sobs as she broke down in the face of his tender concern.

'Oh, Dad!' she said despairingly. 'Look at Andrew!'

'What's wrong? He's a fine, healthy baby,' he assured her, unable to understand what she was referring to.

She shook her head helplessly, her words breaking out in sharp bursts. 'He's the image of Patrick. I'll never forget him now.'

Her bald statement hit Martin Devlin hard. He had dismissed Patrick Hagan out of hand and it took some time to grasp the import of Ruth's words. His expression became very thoughtful and he signalled a nurse to take Andrew away. He put an arm around Ruth's shoulders and she clung to him as she sobbed out her distress. Eventually she calmed down and limply withdrew from him, mopping up her face with tissues. He waited and then attacked the problem, knowing it would do no good to push it away.

'What exactly are your feelings towards Patrick Hagan now, Ruth?'

She shook her head, her lips tightly compressed.

'Come on, now. I'm not going to bite. Let's bring it out into the open. Do you love him, hate him or what?'

'I still love him,' she whispered.

Martin Devlin paused to consider this and then asked dubiously, 'Was I so very wrong about him, Ruth?'

She nodded dumbly and he frowned, puzzled that his judgement could have been badly astray.

'Would you change your mind now if he still wanted to marry you?'

Ruth nodded and then shook her head wearily. 'I don't know, Dad. Besides, there's no way he could want me now. Not after the way I scorned him. I meant to hurt him and I did, very cruelly. There's no way back.' She lay her head back on the pillow and closed her eyes.

Martin Devlin felt an acute sense of failure. He had never understood his daughter's involvement with Patrick Hagan, and he struggled to come to grips with it. He was not a man to face failure easily. 'You must write to him, Ruth,' he declared, seeing that as the only solution.

Her eyes fluttered open, startled by his words.

'You must write to him and tell him about Andrew. If he's anything of the man you think he is, he'll burn a trail to your doorstep.'

'I wouldn't want that, Dad, not for him to come because of Andrew.' She gave him a watery smile. 'Don't mind me just now. I'll get over it. This silly emotional weakness is post-natal depression. The doctor says so.'

Her father looked at her gravely and said, 'Ruth, no man worth his salt would want to be left in ignorance about his own son. Write to him and see what happens. One way or another you'll be left in no doubt as to Patrick Hagan's feelings towards you.'

'We'll see,' she murmured. Then wanting to change the subject she asked, 'Have you been doing any sightseeing?'

Her father reluctantly took the hint, answering her question and talking of other mundane matters. Only as he was leaving did he refer back to the problem. 'Give that letter some thought, Ruth. Loose ends are very untidy. They keep nagging.'

He was right. She did not imagine that Patrick

could possibly want her again, but maybe it was wrong of her to keep the knowledge of his child from him. He had said he wanted a family, and if he never married, Andrew might be his only child. She should write to him, and if he was interested . . . if he came . . . maybe . . .

She tried to disregard the hope which wormed around her heart trying to take hold. In the weeks which followed Ruth wrote many letters to Patrick and posted none of them. As much as she tried to keep an appeal out of her words, she could always read it between the lines. She had no right to make any appeal to him, after that cruel rejection. It was not until she and Andrew were settled into her house at Tergola that she finally achieved a message which could only be interpreted as precisely that, a factual statement. She read it over once more to be absolutely sure.

Dear Patrick,
  Our son was born on the 28th of September. I have named him Andrew. Please understand that I accept full responsibility for him and I make no claim on you whatsoever. I am informing you of Andrew's birth because you once expressed a desire to have children and I thought you had the right to know that you have a son.
                              Yours sincerely,
                              Ruth Devlin

It said enough and no more. Ruth sealed the letter into an envelope, addressed it, and slipped out to post it while Andrew was still having his morning sleep. Even at the letterbox she hesitated, wondering if she was doing the right thing. Then with a spurt of determination she shoved it down the slot and turned away. She had followed her conscience. It was up to Patrick now. All she could do was wait.

The weeks rolled on towards Christmas. There was no response to her letter. Ruth's tension eased, replaced by a dull passivity. The hope which had struggled to live died a painful death. She buried it under preparations for Christmas. At least she had her baby to share it with.

CHAPTER TEN

THE persistent buzz of the telephone nagged her awake. She stumbled out of bed, suddenly alarmed that anyone would ring at such an hour. There was an irritable cry from Andrew and Ruth quickly snatched up the handset, not wanting him to be disturbed.

'Hello,' she said anxiously.

'Ruth, is that you?'

Shock rippled through her, making her gasp as she recognised the voice. 'Patrick?' she asked incredulously.

'Yes. I've just got home from Europe and found your letter waiting for me. May I come and visit you? I'd like, very much, to see the child,' he said, his voice distant and impersonal.

The sheer unexpectedness of his call and his request had Ruth reeling. 'When?' she blurted out.

'I have a few arrangements to make. Say a couple of days.'

Ruth was shaken by a surge of emotion which frightened her. She desperately wanted him to come, yet shrank from the turmoil his coming would provoke.

'Is that all right, Ruth?' His voice held a strained note this time.

'Yes. If you're sure you want to come, Patrick,' she said uncertainly.

'I'll telephone when I get to Mascot Airport.'

He hung up, leaving Ruth with a dead receiver in her hand. She replaced it slowly, trying to recall everything he had said. It was obvious that she had underestimated his possible reaction to her letter, since he meant to drop everything and come immediately. Two days, three at the most and he would be here. Just his voice had shaken her, let alone his presence.

She wondered why he had been in Europe, what he had been doing the past year, whether she still meant anything to him. He would surely have tried to erase her from his mind. Only one thing was certain. He urgently wanted to see Andrew. The child was Patrick's son as well as hers, and whatever demands he made she had to keep that fact fairly in mind.

For the rest of the night she tossed and turned, worrying one moment, then longing for his arrival, admitting to herself how much she wanted to see him while fearful of the effect he was bound to have on her life. It was a dilemma which could not be solved until Patrick came, but it teased her mind endlessly.

Andrew's crying woke her the next morning. Ruth's eyes felt gravelly from lack of sleep. She staggered to the bassinet and brought the baby back to bed with her. As he gurgled up at her the resemblance to Patrick in his little face became more definite and heart-wrenching.

'Little do you know, my love, that your father's coming to see you very soon. I wonder what he'll think of you.'

Andrew screwed up his face and gave a lusty yell,

reminding her that he was not there for conversation but for mother's milk.

She grinned down at him and murmured, 'All right, you demanding little monster,' and pushed her nightie aside to fulfil his needs.

It was a difficult day for her. She threw herself into housework until every room was spotless and then spent the afternoon shopping. Unsure of what Patrick's plans might be when he arrived, she wanted to be prepared for any contingency. She found herself scanning the supermarket shelves for delicacies and chided herself for being foolish. It was far more sensible to keep everything as normal as possible.

The next day she had nothing to do, and Andrew became fretful, sensing his mother's anxiety. She ended up taking him for a drive in the car and was half an hour away from home when the thought struck her that Patrick might catch an earlier flight. She might miss his call. She knew he would call again, but she hurried home, not wanting a minute to be lost. Afternoon dragged into evening. She finally went to bed in an attempt to sleep the hours away.

The telephone woke her at six-thirty in the morning. She flew out of bed to answer it and stifled a sigh of relief when Patrick's voice came over the wire.

'Ruth, I'm at Mascot now. I don't want to waste time on the telephone. Would you please ring around and book me into a local motel?' he said abruptly.

'For how long, Patrick?' she asked smoothly, feeling the blood palpitating through her veins as she waited for his reply.

'Say two weeks. That should be long enough one

way or another,' he answered tiredly, and it was impossible for Ruth to gauge what he meant by that comment. 'If you'll do that I'll get on my way.'

'Very well. I'll see you later,' she said, careful to keep any hint of excitement out of her voice.

'Yes,' he said briefly and hung up.

Ruth was galvanised into action. She showered and washed her hair, donned a house-wrap and made her bed. She could hear Andrew rattling his beads across his bassinet and went to get him up, smiling as he lifted his arms up to her.

'Oh, I hope your father is going to love you,' she crooned at him, hugging him tightly.

There was so much to do. She fed Andrew and dressed him in a little playsuit, proud of his brown, sturdy body, glad he was such a happy baby. His interested eyes followed her as she pulled on a cool, blue, button-through sundress. After several telephone calls she finally managed to book Patrick into a nearby motel. Then she carried Andrew out to the kitchen and laid him in a bouncinette while she had some breakfast.

Her eyes kept glancing at the clock, and tension tore at her nerves as the minutes ticked past. A car drew up in the street outside, but Ruth steadfastly refused to look out of the window, unwilling to be disappointed. When the doorbell rang her heart stopped for a moment. Then she picked up Andrew, sat him on her hip and went to greet his father.

Patrick's gaze moved slowly from mother to child and back again as Ruth absorbed the shock of his appearance. He was thinner, his face haggard with weariness and his once-black hair was liberally streaked with grey.

'Hello, Patrick.' The words came out as little more than a whisper and she forced more volume into her voice. 'Won't you come in?'

He hesitated, glancing down at his suitcase.

'You can put it in the hall,' she nodded.

'Thank you. You look well, Ruth.'

'You look exhausted. Come and sit down,' she invited, leading the way into the living-room.

'Thanks, but I'd rather stretch my legs. It's been a long trip,' he remarked stiffly.

'Would you like some coffee?' she asked, trying to project a calmness she did not feel.

'Thank you,' he nodded politely.

She bent to put Andrew in the bouncinette but he forestalled her.

'May I hold him for a while? I'll be careful.'

She silently passed Andrew to him. Patrick turned away and walked over to the picture window, gazing at his son, who was clearly suspicious of this stranger. Ruth saw the beginning of a smile on Patrick's face and then busied herself in the kitchen. When she came out with the coffee Andrew was laughing and waving his hands excitedly and Patrick grinned his pleasure at her.

'He's beautiful!' he declared warmly.

Ruth smiled. 'I think so. Shall I take him while you have your coffee?'

Patrick nodded and she laid Andrew in the bouncinette. He kicked his legs and blew bubbles, demanding their attention. Patrick chuckled and knelt down, tickling Andrew's tummy, making him squirm in delight. Painful emotion choked Ruth as she watched the two of them together. Patrick glanced up and caught the tense expression on her face and his own became shuttered.

'Thank you for letting me know, Ruth. I appreciate what it must have cost you to write to me,' he said quietly.

She looked away, unable to hold his gaze without revealing how much his presence meant to her. She sat down, pulling her coffee towards her and stirring it distractedly.

'Your coffee will be cold if you don't come and drink it,' she said to cover the awkward silence between them. He sat in the opposite armchair and reached for the sugar. 'I booked you in at the Seaview Motel. It's only a couple of blocks away. I hope you'll be comfortable there,' she prattled on, her whole mind and body in upheaval at having him near her.

'Thank you,' he nodded and picked up his cup of coffee. He sipped it for a while, watching Andrew with hooded eyes. 'You sounded surprised when I telephoned the other night.' His gaze switched to her, sharply inquiring. 'Didn't you think I'd come, Ruth?'

She flushed and gave a non-committal shrug. 'I didn't know how you'd react, Patrick. When you didn't acknowledge my letter I assumed you weren't interested.'

'My God! Not interested!' he muttered grimly. 'And were you glad about that?'

The bitterness in his voice and the accusing look in his eyes squeezed her heart. Her hopes for a reconciliation faded. His resentment went too deep.

'No,' she said quietly. 'I accepted it, that's all. What you do with your life is your business, Patrick.'

His lips twisted cynically. 'Yes, that's exactly what you'd think.' He sighed wearily and leaned back in his chair. 'It was a stark little letter, Ruth. It gave me no hint as to whether a visit from me would be welcome or not.'

'Does it matter?' she asked stiffly.

'Oh yes, it matters. You've given me a son, but how much I see of him depends very largely on you, doesn't it?' he said slowly, watching her with probing eyes.

'And on you.' She met his gaze unflinchingly, leaving the challenge for him to pick up.

'Tell me why you wrote, Ruth.'

She looked at Andrew, her face softening as the baby gurgled up at her. 'You're his father. You had the right to know. And Andrew has the right to know his father. It's up to you whether you want to be part of his life or not.'

His silence drew her gaze back to him. He was looking at Andrew, naked yearning on his face.

'Is it all right for me to nurse him?'

The depth of emotion in his voice choked her and she passed him the baby without comment. Patrick cradled him in his arms, rocking him gently.

'He has your eyes.'

'Yes,' she answered briefly, not trusting her voice.

He shot her a discerning look. 'Did you have a hard time with him, Ruth?'

She shook her head. 'No. It was an easy birth.'

A silence fell between them until Ruth noticed that

Andrew was asleep. She took him quietly from Patrick, indicating that he should be put to bed. Ruth dallied in the bedroom, reluctant to return immediately. She needed time to brace herself against the emotional impact of meeting Patrick again. Her imagination had not really prepared her for the reality, the hard edge of his manner towards her, the loving way he had taken to Andrew and the sheer physical pain of seeing them together. She pressed her hand to her heart to slow its rapid beating, then took a deep breath and returned to the living-room.

Patrick's head had lolled sideways, his eyes closed, his breathing heavy, his whole body slack. He looked so tired that Ruth did not attempt to wake him, taking the opportunity to study his face unobserved. He had aged considerably over the past year, the grooves in his cheeks deeper and the skin around his eyes pouched. She wanted to smooth the lines from his face and run her fingers through his greying hair, but she resisted the impulse, taking a seat away from him, just watching him sleep and taking stock of what had happened so far.

There had not yet been enough time to discuss his motive for this visit. Patrick had taken the initiative from her with his questions, revealing little about himself except that he felt strongly about the situation. Andrew seemed to be the focal point of those emotions, and Ruth had to find out what he intended for the future. If he had come only to see his son, the next two weeks would stretch Ruth's nerves to breaking-point and any future visits loomed as a continuing torment. If only Patrick had given one hint of softness towards her she would have leapt at the chance to meet him halfway, but all his tenderness had been for Andrew. Now there was nothing for her to do but erect some necessary defences.

The baby began to whimper and Ruth was startled by the quick passage of time. She went to him quickly before he demanded his lunch in his usual loud way. Hushing him as she picked him up, she took him to her bedroom, unbuttoned her sunfrock and began to feed him. She watched him indulgently, comforted by the thought that at least she had her baby to love.

A sound distracted her attention and she looked up to see Patrick leaning against the doorway. Her involuntary jerk caused Andrew to protest. She hurriedly changed him over to the other breast and threw an appealing glance at Patrick.

'We won't be long.'

Fatigue seemed to have drawn his features tighter, giving him a pale, pinched look. There was an immense weariness in his dark eyes.

'Take your time,' he muttered, but instead of moving away he came and sat on the bed, observing in silence as Andrew took his fill. 'I'm sorry I fell asleep. I wanted to talk with you,' he murmured apologetically.

'There's plenty of time. You must be terribly tired,' she answered quietly and looked up to see him squeeze his forehead between finger and thumb in a telling gesture. 'I'll take you to your motel later and you can have a proper rest,' she added in concern, and he nodded.

Andrew was finally satisfied and she laid him aside while she hastily rearranged her clothes.

'Don't be embarrassed, Ruth,' Patrick said wryly. 'You looked very beautiful suckling your baby.'

She flushed and picked up the baby, using him as a defence. 'I'll get some lunch ready,' she said distractedly, and having put Andrew down in the bassinet she escaped to the kitchen.

Patrick followed her, propping himself on a kitchen stool, watching her silently as she put steaks on to cook and began preparing a salad to go with them. She did not know what to say and his silence was not encouraging.

'Under what name did you register Andrew?' he asked suddenly.

'Devlin.' She glanced at him sharply. 'What else?'

He shrugged. 'It could not have been easy for you.'

Ruth thought she detected concern in his eyes and spoke quickly to erase it, too proud to accept sympathy. 'It was all right, Patrick. I wrote a book. What have you been doing all year?' That was a safe question and she was curious to know.

'Filling in time, just drifting. I went yacht-racing a couple of times, then toured around Europe. When it got too cold I went home. A completely aimless existence, while unbeknownst to me, you were tucked away in Australia having our son,' he finished, and the bitterness in his voice made Ruth wary.

She put the finishing touches to the salad, lifted out the steaks and carried the plates to the diningtable. They ate in silence for a while, both biding their time. It was Patrick who spoke first and his voice was harsh with irony.

'I don't suppose it occurred to you that I might feel responsible.'

'Yes, it occurred to me,' she admitted softly.

'And you couldn't let me know earlier than this?' He tempered the harshness in his voice and added more gently, 'Couldn't you have let me come, Ruth?'

She carefully laid down her knife and fork and faced him squarely. 'I'm sorry, Patrick. It was . . . not an easy time for me. I tried to write earlier but . . . it wasn't easy.'

'I see.' His mouth tightened. 'Well, I'm here. And I'm here to stay, Ruth, and you're just going to have to tolerate my presence, one way or another.'

His eyes were brooding with purpose, and a little shiver crept up Ruth's spine. There was no softness in his eyes for her. He was going to make it hard. There was too much bitterness in him. She sucked in a deep breath and asked, 'What do you mean by that?'

His eyes were diamond-hard. 'It means I want my son, Ruth, my full share of Andrew's life. I want to see him grow up day by day, not occasionally. I want to be a proper father to him, be at hand when he needs me. Are you listening?'

She had closed her eyes, unable to bear the cold speculation in Patrick's. There was nothing for her in his claims. It was all Andrew, and the disappointment was too savage to let him see.

'Yes,' she murmured.

'No comment?'

'You haven't finished.'

'The answer is obvious.'

'Say it,' she persisted.

'The most satisfactory way of achieving the situation I want is for us to be married.'

He waited for a reaction but there was none. The reasons he stated for his proposal all centred on Andrew, and the slim hope Ruth had cherished for something different was being crushed by despair. It was impossible to speak without betraying her inner pain.

'I am well aware that you have no personal wish to marry me,' he continued tersely. 'Your words and actions have been more than eloquent in convincing me of that. However, all personal emotions aside, I hope you will consider the advantages in a marriage of convenience. I won't place any demands on you. You'll be completely free to do whatever you want. In fact, more free than you are at the moment, since I will be here to look after Andrew and support both of you.'

He paused and Ruth inserted bitterly, 'What about your own freedom, Patrick?'

He gave a harsh laugh. 'Freedom to do what?'

She looked at him with all the memory of disillusionment in her eyes. He shook his head and his voice softened.

'Whatever else you imagined, Ruth, the simple truth was that you were all I wanted then. The only freedom I want now is the freedom to love and care for my son.' A bleak desolation settled on his face and he added tiredly, 'I'm almost forty. Andrew is my only child. I've travelled the whole empty world and the only magic in it is right here. Please credit me with enough intelligence to know what I want, and mean what I say.'

Ruth searched his brooding eyes and could not doubt the sincerity of his words. She had to believe him, but whether she could sustain such a surface relationship with him was another matter altogether.

'I need time to think about it,' she said bluntly.

He nodded. 'Take your time. I'm in no hurry for an answer. I'm not going anywhere. I'm here to stay, Ruth, whether you accept my proposition or not.'

She looked at him blankly, still confused by the emotions he had stirred. 'What do you mean by that?'

'I intend to apply for Australian citizenship whatever you decide. If you find the idea of our marriage too distasteful, I'll buy a house nearby so that Andrew can visit me and I can take an interest in him. I don't think you'll begrudge me that much,' he added coldly.

The blood drained from her face as Ruth understood the trap closing around her. She found herself clenching and unclenching her fists under the table and strove to calm her nerves.

'And have Andrew torn between the two of us?'

'That's your choice,' he said deliberately, hard purpose darkening his eyes. He pushed his chair back and stood up. 'Thanks for the lunch, Ruth. I'm afraid I had little appetite. If you'll direct me to the motel I'll go now and get some rest.'

'I'll drive you,' she offered, forcing herself to stand on shaky legs.

'Should you leave Andrew?'

'He'll be all right. I'll only be ten minutes, and I'll ask my neighbour to keep an eye on the baby.'

There was nothing left to say, and she fetched her car keys and took him to the motel.

'I'll call around tomorrow morning if that is convenient to you,' he said smoothly before getting out.

She nodded and watched him as he strode away from her, silently despairing of his ever coming to her with love in his heart. Patrick was probably not aware of it, but he had given her no choice at all. Perhaps his alternative plan of living nearby would have been feasible if she no longer loved him, but Ruth knew she would find that unbearable. Yet to marry him if he no longer loved her was to court disaster in a far more intimate way.

He had loved her once. Maybe with Andrew as a bridge between them he might learn to love her again. She knew she was going to accept his offer. All year she had tried to put him out of her mind and heart, but the yearning for him had only ever been temporarily shelved, always ready to eat at her when her control slipped. Since Andrew's birth that yearning had intensified. Now Patrick was giving her a second chance, a very shaky second chance, but Ruth was going to take it. Whatever else their marriage yielded, she would have him by her side, for better or for worse.

CHAPTER ELEVEN

RUTH was just lifting Andrew out of his bath when the doorbell heralded Patrick's arrival. She wrapped the baby in a large fluffy towel while trying to still the nervous flutter in her heart. Her decision to marry Patrick had not faltered, but she was keenly aware that any personal relationship between them was balanced finely in the innocent hands of their baby son. She cradled Andrew against her shoulder and went to open the door.

Patrick smiled at them. Ruth knew the smile was mainly directed at his son, but it helped soothe her inner anxiety. He was dressed in jeans and a casual sports shirt and he looked more relaxed. The heavy lines of fatigue had lifted and the deep weariness had left his eyes. He looked more like his former self, and Ruth had to struggle against showing her love for him. She pitched her voice to a light, friendly level.

'Come in, Patrick. I was just going to take Andrew out near the pool for his sun-bath. Would you like to join us?'

'If you don't mind,' he replied in a carefully neutral tone.

'Why don't you carry Andrew down while I make us both some coffee?'

'I'd like that,' he nodded and held out his arms for the baby.

The action made touching inevitable, but he took

Andrew quite naturally, giving no sign that her closeness affected him in any way. His attention was all on his son, and he chuckled as the baby blew bubbles at him.

'Thanks, Ruth,' he said casually.

She watched him carry the baby down the back steps, then stepped into the kitchen. She could see them from the window while the percolator heated up. Patrick carefully smoothed the towel over the grass, making sure it was not wrinkled under the baby. He stretched out on the lawn beside his son, his head propped up on one hand. Andrew waved and kicked, enjoying his freedom. A bemused smile softened Patrick's face as he examined the tiny hands and feet. Ruth felt intensely moved by the father-and-son picture they made, and she vowed to do her best to make it a permanent way of life.

As soon as the coffee was ready she loaded mugs and biscuits onto a tray and carried it down. Her breath caught in her throat as Patrick directed a happy grin at her.

'I'm a doting father already.'

She returned the grin. 'Andrew loves to be free of nappies.'

'Who could blame him?'

Ruth set the tray down on the garden table, hoping that Patrick's good humour would not suddenly disappear. She did not want the awful tension of yesterday to return. 'Do you want your coffee there on the lawn?'

'No. I'll join you.'

She sat down on one of the sun-loungers as he stood up. Her legs felt shaky whenever he was close to her. She did not want to betray her feelings, not at this uncertain stage. Patrick strolled the few steps over to the sun-lounger next to hers. He sat down facing her. Neither of them took a mug of coffee or a biscuit.

'Did you sleep well?' she asked, trying to sound natural. Tension was creeping up on her again.

'Yes, surprisingly enough.' A wry smile touched his lips. 'I guess a man can only go so long without sleep. It's been a hectic couple of days.' He looked at her guardedly. 'Your letter threw me into a spin. It was a bare little birth notice, Ruth. No joy, no pain, just here is the news. You can't imagine what I felt.'

Ruth flushed and looked at Andrew, remembering the joy of his birth and the pain of not having Patrick at her side. 'I didn't know how you'd take it, and I didn't want you to think I was asking you for anything.'

'God almighty! You'd borne my child. You had the right to ask me for anything.'

The strangled passion in his voice completely unnerved her. She forced herself to answer, to explain. 'You know that's not so, Patrick, not after I rejected you.'

There was dead silence for so long that Ruth darted a glance at him. He was leaning forward, his elbows on his knees, one hand rubbing at the other. His gaze was fixed on Andrew. He drew in a deep breath and let it slowly shudder out.

'Well, Ruth, you've had time to think about it. Will you give me your answer now?'

The tone of tired resignation told her he expected

another rejection. 'I'll marry you, if that's what you want,' she said quietly, ignoring the heavy lump in her heart.

She saw his throat move in a convulsive swallow but he did not turn back to her. 'Yes. That's what I want,' he said just as quietly. Then he swung his head around and his eyes held a determined challenge. 'I'd like to know what I can expect from you, though, whether it's an armed truce or a willingness to be friends. Hatred and contempt can be pretty difficult to stifle when living in close quarters.'

Pain filled her eyes, impossible to control. 'Is that how you feel towards me?'

'Me?' He was startled out of his guarded expression. His face softened and there was a gleam of vulnerability in his eyes. 'How could I when you've given me such a wonderful gift? I'll do everything in my power to make you and Andrew happy. I was asking if you could be open-minded enough to make it easy.'

His answer gave her the courage to speak up. 'I don't hate you, Patrick, I never did. It took me a long time to come to terms with what happened last year. When I wrote to you I hoped you'd come, but it had to be because you wanted to.' She looked down at her hands, saw her nails biting deeply into the palms and unclenched her fingers. She drew in a deep breath and added, 'I hoped that you might want us to be a family, so you see, I'm more than open-minded. I'll try to be more tolerant this time.'

Silence greeted her answer and she glanced back at him nervously. His expression was difficult to read.

'That's very generous of you, Ruth,' he said at last. 'I thought you might find it difficult to live with me.'

'There is one thing, Patrick,' she murmured. A flush of embarrassment started creeping across her face and she looked at Andrew, too selfconscious to hold Patrick's gaze. 'If we're to be a family, I don't want Andrew to be an only child.'

She heard his sharp intake of breath and could feel his eyes boring into her. His reply was excruciatingly slow in coming.

'You're willing to share your bed with me, Ruth? Have a complete marriage?' The questions were forced out and there was a half-incredulous note in his voice.

'You don't want that?' she asked huskily, a savage desperation wrenching at her heart.

'God, yes!' It was an explosion of relief. 'I just didn't expect . . . I thought . . .' He thrust his fingers through his hair, making a confusion of the unruly curls. 'I thought you would reject me, that you were only accepting me as Andrew's father.'

She shook her head and took her courage a step further. 'I don't think the other way would work very well. It would lead to frustration and misunderstandings. If you really want to share your life with us, then I'd like to share everything as far as possible.'

'You've thought this out, Ruth? Don't promise something you can't give. It's easier to refrain from a physical relationship than be repulsed,' he explained cautiously.

She paled at the reference to her bitter words of last year. 'It's what I want,' she replied firmly.

'When would you like to get married? How much time do you need?'

'I don't need any time. We could go to the Jirrong Courthouse and sign the necessary papers this afternoon, if you like.'

'You don't want a church wedding?'

'No. You do realise it will still be a month before we can marry.'

'Yes, I remember. I'm quite content to wait a month, longer if necessary. I want you to be very sure you know what you're doing. It's one thing to make a decision, and quite another to live with it. A month will give you time to get used to having me around.'

'Do you want to stay here with us?' she asked hesitantly.

'No. Better to take things gradually, but I'd like to meet your parents as soon as possible. If we go into Jirrong this afternoon, could we visit them?'

She darted him a look of surprise, but he appeared to be quite sincere. 'Yes, I think so. Dad's retired and they don't go out much, but I'd better telephone to make sure.' She stood up. 'It's time to take Andrew in, anyway.'

She gathered up the baby and Patrick followed her up the steps and right into Andrew's bedroom. He watched her put him down to sleep and stayed watching him while she telephoned. After a considerable number of surprised comments and a few cautious enquiries, Ruth's mother invited them to dinner. Ruth hung up and sighed. It was not going to be an easy meal. The testing ground of her parents' interest would probably create more tension between her and Patrick. Several hurdles had been crossed, but their relationship was still very strained.

'Is it okay?' Patrick asked sharply and she swung around to face him.

'Yes. We're invited to stay to dinner.'

'You look disturbed.'

She shrugged. 'My parents will be concerned, Patrick.'

He nodded understandingly. 'I want to reassure them.'

'My father . . .' she hesitated, making an agitated gesture with her hand.

'Is hostile? That's to be expected,' he said softly.

'No, not exactly hostile, but . . .'

'Look, let's get this clear, Ruth.' He walked over to her and placed his hands gently on her shoulders, his eyes searching hers anxiously. 'I didn't come here to create problems for you but to try to remove them, make life easier for you. I know your parents are important to you. I realise they can't possibly have a good impression of me, but I want to try to correct that. We have to start somewhere.'

'Thank you,' she whispered huskily, tears swimming into her eyes.

For one hypnotic moment she thought he was going to kiss her. His hands tightened their hold and there was a perceptible, downward tilt of his head. A hungry flame flickered briefly in his eyes and then it was quenched. He pulled back and glanced at his watch.

'I'd better get moving. Can you put your hands on the papers you'll need, birth certificate, etc?'

'Yes.'

'When do you suggest we leave?'

'One-thirty?'

'Right. I'll be dressed and organised and back here by then.'

Before she could draw breath he had left. Ruth shivered as the heat drained out of her veins. She had wanted the security of his arms around her, the warmth of his mouth on hers. Why had he faltered? Did he still think she would reject him? What were his feelings towards her? When she had asked him he had given an indirect answer, tying her emotionally to Andrew as the mother of his son. Certainly he was showing consideration and seemed intent on building a solid relationship. For that much she was intensely grateful. But she wished he had kissed her.

Still, progress had been made, and it was with a lighter heart that Ruth searched through her box of papers for the certificates she needed for this afternoon. She had lunch, woke Andrew and gave him his midday feed, then dressed them both in fresh, attractive clothes. There was a slight flush on her cheeks and her eyes were shining with new hope when she met Patrick at the door at one-thirty. She looked her surprise at his conventional suit and tie.

'Am I too formally dressed?' he asked sharply.

'No, not at all. I just wasn't expecting it. You usually dress in trendy clothes.'

His lips tightened into a thin line, and too late Ruth remembered the scornful accusations she had thrown at him last year.

'I'm ready if you'll bring Andrew's carry-cot for me,' she said hurriedly, angry at herself for being so tactless.

'Of course.'

He brushed past her and picked up the basket, smiling at Andrew who gurgled up at him.

'Does he travel well?'

'He usually sleeps as soon as the car's in motion.'

Ruth locked up the house and led the way to the station-wagon, opening its back door for Patrick to settle the carry-cot on the seat. She offered him the keys but he declined, saying that she knew the way. As she drove he asked questions about her parents and the rest of her family, gradually drawing from her a picture of their lives.

Their business at the courthouse took considerable time with the filling out of various forms. They were given a list of local celebrants with whom they could arrange to perform the ceremony. It was three-thirty and Andrew was getting restive by the time they arrived at the Devlin's home. There was a grim set to Patrick's face as he lifted the carry-cot out of the car, and Ruth impulsively linked her arm with his. His swift glance revealed uncertainty.

'It's all right,' she assured him. 'They only want my happiness.'

'So do I, Ruth. I mean that.'

'Then you have nothing to worry about,' she smiled.

Tuffy suddenly pelted up the front path, doing her usual imitation of a fierce watchdog until she recognised Ruth. Then she danced a frenetic welcome, interspersed with an occasional wary bark at Patrick.

'I swear she thinks she's a Great Dane,' Ruth

laughed as they walked down to the front door. 'Are you good with dogs, Patrick?'

His mood lightened a little. 'I've never been bitten by one.'

'Well, don't be offended if Tuffy jumps on you. She's effectively queen of the house, even though Mum pretends to scold her.' Her mother was waiting at the door, holding it open for them to come straight in. 'Thanks, Mum. Put the carry-cot on the floor, Patrick, and I'll pick Andrew up.'

Martin Devlin made his appearance and Tuffy fluttered excitedly around everyone's legs. Ruth lifted the baby up out of harm's way and smiled at her parents.

'Mum and Dad, I hope we haven't put you out by coming at such short notice, but Patrick was impatient to meet you.'

'Not at all. I'm very pleased to meet you, Mr Hagan,' her father intoned heavily as he offered his hand.

'Probably not as pleased as I am, Mr Devlin, Mrs Devlin,' he replied seriously, taking their hands in turn.

Joyce Devlin bustled them in to the lounge, her hands fluttering nervously until they were all seated. 'You must be wanting a cup of tea,' she declared, and without waiting for an answer, took herself and Tuffy to the kitchen.

Ruth sighed. Her mother's panacea for all the ills did not quite cover this situation, but it was her way of saying welcome. Ruth glanced apprehensively at her father, hoping that he would be generous in his welcome too. He was studiously lighting his pipe.

After a few determined puffs he directed a stern gaze to Patrick, the sharp blue eyes not even wavering slightly in Ruth's direction.

'I understand from Ruth's phone call that you wish to marry my daughter, Mr Hagan.'

Ruth's stomach tightened. Her father's formality was a bad sign. She glanced quickly at Patrick. He returned her father's gaze steadfastly, his expression one of serious intent.

'Yes, I do.'

'For Andrew's sake?'

Patrick hesitated, then picked his words carefully. 'Andrew is my son, Mr Devlin, and I want to be his father in every sense of the word. He's very special to me.'

'And Ruth? Is she special to you?'

Her heart stopped. She held her breath and waited, unable to look at either of them.

'From the first moment we met Ruth has been special to me. She had only to call me at any time and I would have flown to her side. I regret, very much, that she didn't feel able to before this. I hope I can make her feel more secure now that she's given me a second chance.'

Ruth's heart was now racing. She looked searchingly at Patrick, wanting to believe he meant those words, wanting to believe what they suggested. His attention was concentrated on her father, but his expression seemed to be sincere. Her father frowned and waved his pipe.

'It would seem to me, in the light of what happened last year, that such a hasty decision is not wise.'

'Dad, please,' Ruth jumped in, anxious for him not to interfere.

The eyes he turned to her were full of concern. 'Ruth, it's your whole future you're deciding. Patrick Hagan turns up one day and you're marrying him the next. Can't you wait and test how you feel? Your mother and I don't want to see you go through another year like this one. You're hardly back on your feet now, and . . .'

'Stop!' Ruth was on her feet, Andrew clasped tightly against her shoulder. Her eyes darted apprehensively from one man to the other. 'That was my decision last year, not Patrick's, as well you know, Dad. And this is my decision. I'm going to marry Patrick and if it's another mistake, I'll live with it. The matter is not up for discussion.' Andrew began to cry, upset by his mother's agitation. She hushed him impatiently. 'The marriage is set for a month's time and I am not going to change my mind.'

'You were just as sure as that last year, Ruth,' her father said pointedly. 'You wouldn't wait then, and we had to watch you crawl away like a hurt animal to lick your wounds alone.'

'Ruth?'

The soft query was almost an intake of breath. It threw Ruth into a panic. Her father had revealed too much. Patrick was leaning forward, eyes sharply probing, a puzzled crease drawing his eyebrows together.

'That's over,' she declared hurriedly, then turned to her father with even more urgency. 'That's over, Dad. Please. It's my life.'

For a moment it seemed he was going to challenge her claim, but he sighed and lifted his hands in a resigned gesture. 'A month, Ruth. It's not enough when you're considering a lifetime,' he persisted in a quiet, reasoning tone. 'Won't you take more time, not only for yours, but for Andrew's sake.'

'No.' It was a vehement shake of the head.

'Why not?'

'You know why not. It's decided. We've lodged the papers already,' Ruth added with stubborn defiance. She could not look at Patrick.

Martin Devlin stroked his chin, eyeing them both with obvious reservations. 'Well, I hope to God you know what you're doing this time,' he finally declared.

'Here you are!' Joyce Devlin announced, wheeling in a traymobile laden with tea-things, including a large sponge cake replete with cream and strawberries.

Ruth privately blessed her mother. She could not have made a more timely entrance. Ruth's nerves were ragged, and she did not want to look at her father or Patrick. Both men were too perceptive for her peace of mind.

'Well, Joyce, undoubtedly you'll be happy to hear they're getting married in a month's time,' Martin observed drily.

'I told you so, Martin. As soon as I heard you were here, Patrick . . . I can call you Patrick, can't I? and you must call me Joyce . . . anyhow, I knew you'd want to marry Ruth. After all, you wouldn't have come otherwise. I made you black coffee because I remembered in the kitchen that Americans drink coffee instead of tea. And there's cream in the jug if you want it.'

'Thank you. I do prefer coffee,' Patrick smiled, looking a little swamped by Joyce Devlin's ready acceptance of him.

Ruth's father was prompted to a wry comment. 'It's part of my wife's beautiful nature that she accepts things without question.'

'Well, it's no use interfering, Martin. They'll do what they want to do regardless of anything you say. I'll take Andrew while you have your tea, Ruth,' she offered, holding out her arms for him. 'He's lovely, isn't he, Patrick?'

'He certainly is,' Patrick agreed warmly.

'You couldn't possibly go away and leave him.'

'Quite impossible. He looked me in the eye and enslaved me for life,' Patrick grinned. 'Of course I must admit he has the advantage of inheriting Ruth's eyes.'

Joyce laughed delightedly and looked down at the baby with grandmotherly prejudice. 'Yes, he has, but I rather fancy it's your nose. Now tell me about your plans.'

Ruth looked uncertainly at Patrick, but he plunged ahead, his natural charm coming to the fore under her mother's open encouragement.

'We haven't really discussed concrete plans, but I'd like to buy some land around here, enough for Andrew to have a horse, dogs, any pets he'd like. I want him to have all the things I missed out on. Ruth and I can design a house to suit our needs. What do you think, Ruth?'

'I'd like that,' she answered selfconsciously.

Joyce Devlin beamed her delight. 'Oh, I'm so glad you're staying here. I don't see much of Paul and Helen, and I'd really miss Ruth if you took her away. Now, you haven't had a piece of my cake, Patrick. Give him a slice, Ruth.'

Ruth knew Patrick preferred savoury to sweet things, but he accepted a large wedge without demur, an amused twinkle in his eye.

'Delicious!' he pronounced without hesitation. 'Best cake I've ever tasted.'

'Oh, you've probably never had home-made. Bought cakes don't taste as good,' Joyce said smugly.

Her father sighed as Ruth handed him a plate with a generous helping. 'And you wonder that I'm putting on weight.'

Joyce sniffed. 'You know perfectly well that you don't exercise enough, Martin, sitting over those stamps. Now Patrick could do with some weight on. You look a bit on the thin side. I suppose it's all that tripping around, not eating proper meals. You'll have to feed him up, Ruth.'

Patrick almost choked on his cake. So did Ruth. She swallowed hard and blinked back tears before smiling at her mother.

'I think his son has first priority at the moment. I'd better take him, Mum. It's past four o'clock.'

Her mother stood up, still keeping hold of the baby. 'I'll come with you. The men can have a nice chat by themselves.'

Oh God! A nice chat! Ruth thought despairingly. She threw a hard, warning look at her father and accompanied her mother to a bedroom.

'He's nice, Ruth, really nice,' her mother declared as soon as they were settled.

'I'm glad you like him. I hope Dad comes around.'

'Oh, don't worry about your father. He gets a bit hot-headed now and then, but it never lasts. I can soften him, and really, he's soft as butter underneath. I'd say your Patrick's just the same.'

'Would you, Mum?'

'Goodness yes. Look how he wants to please you. He must love you very much.'

The thought disturbed Ruth's mind. Patrick did seem to want to please her, cautious about asking what she wanted and considering her desires before his own, particularly today. He had only been forceful on the question of marriage, but once she had accepted him, his concern had all been for her needs. Could he still love her? He had declared that he would have come if only she had called. Had he been speaking the truth, and if so, was her mother right? Her heart ached for his love. The uncertainty in her mind was too much of a torment. Tonight she would ask him straight out what his feelings were.

Andrew contentedly went to sleep after his feed. Ruth followed her mother back out to the lounge, worrying over what had been discussed in her absence. Patrick and her father were conversing quite naturally on a first-name basis and she breathed a sigh of relief.

The usual homely atmosphere prevailed, and continued to do so right through dinner. She noticed that Patrick seemed not to talk about himself, but rather showed an avid interest in everything to do with her family, as if he was soaking in a completely new lifestyle.

'You must come to Paul's with us for Christmas,' Joyce finally declared. 'Would you mind sharing him, Ruth? He has to meet the family sometime, and I'm sure Patrick would enjoy it.'

He looked at her for a decision, not pressing either way.

'It's up to you,' she said uncertainly.

'I'd like to go, if you don't mind.'

'Then we'll go.'

'We can go shopping again,' he smiled.

'Again? Have you already been Christmas shopping?' Joyce asked in surprise.

'No, I tagged along with Ruth last year. In fact I pressed my company on her. She thought Christmas shopping would bore me to the point of distraction, but I loved every minute of it.'

There was a warm caress in his eyes as he shared the memory. The unexpectedness of it confused Ruth for a moment. Then in quick response she smiled back, her heart giving a joyous little leap as hope climbed on hope.

'Would you believe, Mum, he'd never been Christmas shopping? He played with that silly electronic game for half an hour and insisted that I buy it for the boys.'

'They loved it!' Joyce exclaimed. 'Oh, it's going to be a lovely Christmas this year, what with Andrew and everything.'

'And speaking of Andrew, we must get him home, Patrick. Then I can settle him for the night after I feed him. It's already eight-thirty.' And she was impatient to get Patrick alone. All her silent yearning could no longer be denied. She had to know.

'I must thank you both for your kindness,' Patrick said with obvious sincerity, his eyes glowing warmly at Ruth's parents. 'I was very apprehensive about this meeting, and you've made me feel at home. It means a great deal to me.'

'That's very sweet of you, Patrick,' Joyce smiled, 'but naturally Ruth's home will be your home. We're both very happy to welcome you into our family, aren't we, Martin?'

'Yes. Yes, we are. As usual Joyce is right. I don't know why I ever doubt her,' he teased, patting her affectionately on the knee.

'Because you like to think you know better,' she laughed and stood up. 'I'll get the baby, Ruth.'

Patrick took the carry-cot from her mother and Ruth went ahead to open doors. Her parents flanked Patrick as he followed her and she felt elated that the liking seemed mutual. Her parents, at least, would present no more problems. Goodbyes were exchanged and at last she and Patrick were alone.

CHAPTER TWELVE

'THEY'RE wonderful people, your parents, Ruth. You can feel the love in their home. I wish . . .' He paused, then sighed and fell silent.

Ruth took her eyes off the road and glanced sharply at him. His body looked relaxed but there was a tight, closed expression on his face. She wished the drive home was over so that she could concentrate solely on him, but the opportunity to draw him out had just been handed to her.

'What do you wish, Patrick?'

'Oh, about a thousand things,' he replied in a wry drawl. 'It doesn't matter, Ruth. It was good of them to accept me like that.'

He was thinking of her parents. Was he remembering last year when he had not wanted to meet them, even been afraid of their influence on her?

'Dad was a bit difficult,' she said hesitantly, still worrying over what he might have said to Patrick out of her hearing.

Patrick made no reply. She darted an anxious glance at him. He was frowning heavily.

'Patrick?'

His head jerked around, his gaze dark and brooding.

Ruth shrank back inside herself, her courage

dwindling. 'Oh, nothing,' she mumbled and returned her attention to the road.

The silence stretched her nerves all the way home. Her mind was a turmoil of urgency, yet the right words would not form. Patrick did not help. He was no longer relaxed. She could feel tension emanating from him. He did not speak at all, even when the car stopped. He alighted swiftly and reached into the back seat for Andrew's carry-cot. It was as if he was in a hurry to get away.

Ruth walked ahead and unlocked the front door. Patrick carried Andrew into the bedroom. The baby was still asleep and Ruth did not disturb him. Time with Patrick was more important than the night feed just now. That could wait. She had to stop Patrick from going. She followed him out of the bedroom and closed the door. Before she could say anything he turned to her, strain showing clearly on his face.

'Ruth . . .'

'Don't go.'

'I must . . .'

'No, please.'

'Ruth, I must talk to you.'

'Oh!' She sighed her relief and gave him a shaky smile. 'I'm sorry. I thought you were going and I need to talk to you. Do you want a drink?'

'No.' There was a grim, determined line about his mouth, but his eyes held an agony of doubt. 'Could we just sit down and talk for a while? There are a few things I'd like to get straight.'

He took her elbow and steered her into an armchair, but he did not sit down. His body was tense. He turned aside, raking his thick, unruly curls with agitated fingers. He paced a few steps away from her, shaking his head.

'It doesn't add up, Ruth. I could hardly believe your manner to me today, but this afternoon . . .' He turned and shot out an upturned palm in impatient appeal. 'Your father said . . .' He paused, his eyes probing hers with sharp intensity. 'What happened this year, Ruth? I know you said it wasn't easy for you. I thought you meant being pregnant with my child. But it must have been more than that. Your father said "a hurt animal" and he was concerned. As if he thought I could hurt you . . . hurt you badly.'

At first she could not understand his puzzlement, but clearly there was a struggle with disbelief on his face. 'How could you think that I . . . that I walked away from last year unscarred? It was like a death.'

'But you despised me, Ruth. Your words, your face that night . . . the letter . . . Oh God! that cold, little letter!' He closed his eyes and pain deepened the lines on his face. 'Nine months of carrying my child and not a word to me.'

A sickening wave of guilt sucked at her heart. 'I'm sorry, Patrick. You did say you didn't want anything to remind you of me. I thought you'd just go on with . . . with your life,' she finished limply.

'My life!' It was a breath of derision and his eyes gently mocked her. 'Did you really think I could forget you, Ruth? That week together was the only time I ever lived. You gave me life, a reason for being . . . and I'm here because any crumbs you let drop from your table are better than nothing at all.'

She shook her head, hardly able to take in the

incredible things he was saying. But she could not disbelieve. The suffering was there, impossible to reject. 'I never stopped loving you,' she whispered, and her eyes showed all the painful torment of the past year.

'Oh my God, no!' It was a cry of anguish. His eyes begged her to deny it. 'All this time,' he pleaded. 'Ruth!'

'I'm sorry. I'm sor . . .'

Her cry was stifled against his chest as he swept her up into a possessive embrace.

'Hush! Just let me hold you. You don't know how much I've craved for the feel of your body next to mine. Oh, Ruth, Ruth.' It was a groan of longing, and his hands ran over her feverishly, as if he could not touch enough of her.

Ruth pressed as close as she could, glorying in the marvellous sensation of being where she belonged, in the arms of the man she loved. It was wonderful to slide her hands under his coat and up over the taut muscles of his back. She could feel the pounding of his heart and knew it was pounding for her. And everything was all right. It was all right. They were home together, at last.

He rubbed his cheek against her hair and his breath was warm on her temples. She lifted her face and kissed his throat, a lingering, savouring kiss.

'Ruth,' he murmured, and it was a throb of love.

He gently pulled her head back and his kiss was soft with a sweetness which melted her bones. She clung to him and gradually the kiss grew more fervent. There was a long hunger to be appeased and a year's bitter suffering to be swept away. The warm tide of passion gathered force, stirring, demanding closer intimacy.

'Ruth.' It was a cry of need.

'Yes,' the only possible answer. 'Oh, yes.'

And then there was a time of beautiful loving when they could not have enough of each other, and their bodies spoke the words of need answering need far more eloquently than any voice.

It was a loud wail from Andrew which finally broke their total absorption in each other.

'Our son is calling,' Patrick whispered huskily.

'Our son. Can you forgive me, Patrick?'

The soft plea was silenced by another kiss.

'I have you again, and him. It's all I want. And this time there'll be no mistakes, Ruth, I promise you. I've left that world behind. It lost any attraction it ever had when you walked out on me. We'll make a world of our own.'

'I said such dreadful things to you.'

He placed a gentle finger on her lips. 'All true, my darling. You held up an image of me and forced me to look at it, and I learned to despise it too over those long, empty months. I was on my way back to you to try again when I got your letter.'

'Oh no! Oh, Patrick! I filled wastepaper bins with letters I didn't post.'

'What did they say?'

'They said I needed you. I needed you so desperately.'

And he kissed her again to answer her need, and she wound her arms around him, hugging him to her with all the joyful satisfaction of possession.

A more belligerent cry from Andrew insisted on attention.

Patrick grinned down at her. 'Shall I go and get him and bring him in here?'

'Why not?' she smiled back at him. 'We're a family, aren't we?'

'Yes. Our very own.'

And there was such blissful contentment in his voice, Ruth felt like crying. But she didn't. The time for tears was past, and the future shone ahead, far too brightly for any tears, not even tears of happiness.

Harlequin Presents

Coming Next Month

927 AN ELUSIVE MISTRESS Lindsay Armstrong
An interior designer from Brisbane finally finds a man to share the rest of her life with—only to have her ex-husband return and reawaken feelings she'd thought were hidden forever.

928 ABODE OF PRINCES Jayne Bauling
In mysterious Rajasthan, Fate prompts a young woman to redefine her understanding of love and friendship. But the man she meets and loves will hear nothing of her breaking her engagement for him.

929 POPPY GIRL Jaqueline Gilbert
Dreams of wealth don't overwhelm a prospective heiress. But a certain Frenchman does. If only she didn't come to suspect his motives for sweeping her off her feet.

930 LOVE IS A DISTANT SHORE Claire Harrison
A reporter with a knack for getting to the heart of the matter disturbs the concentration of a young woman planning to swim Lake Ontario. Surely she should concentrate on one goal at a time.

931 CAPABLE OF FEELING Penny Jordan
In sharing a roof to help care for her boss's niece and nephew, a young woman comes to terms with her inability to express love. Is it too late to change the confines of their marriage agreement?

932 VILLA IN THE SUN Marjorie Lewty
Villa Favorita is the private paradise she shared with her husband—until his fortunes plummeted and he drove her away. Now she has been asked to handle the sale. Little does she know how closely her husband follows the market.

933 LAND OF THUNDER Annabel Murray
The past is a blank to this accident victim. She feels a stranger to her "husband." Worse, their new employer touches something disturbing within her. Something's terribly wrong here.

934 THE FINAL PRICE Patricia Wilson
In Illyaros, where her Greek grandfather lies ill, her ex-husband denies both their divorce and her right to remarry. Yet he was unfaithful to her! No wonder she hasn't told him about the birth of their son.

Available in November wherever paperback books are sold, or through Harlequin Reader Service:

In the U.S.
P.O. Box 1397
Buffalo, N.Y.
14240-1397

In Canada
P.O. Box 2800, Postal Station A
5170 Yonge Street
Willowdale, Ontario M2N 6J3

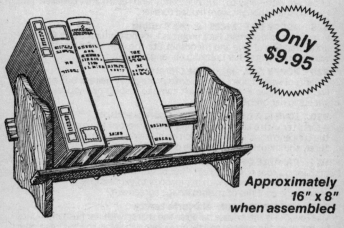

Take 4 novels and a surprise gift FREE

HARLEQUIN HISTORICAL

Explore love with Harlequin in the Middle Ages, the Renaissance, in the Regency, the Victorian and other eras.

Relive within these books the endless ages of romance, set against authentic historical backgrounds. Two new historical love stories published each month.

HIST-A-1